FOR THE RECORD

For Mum and Dad, the World's Best.

Ellie Irving

FOR THE RECORD

How we saved our village
with dedication and doughnuts

CORGI BOOKS

FOR THE RECORD
A CORGI BOOK 978 0 552 56359 8

First published in Great Britain by The Bodley Head,
an imprint of Random House Children's Publishers UK
A Random House Group Company

The Bodley Head edition published 2011
This edition published 2012

1 3 5 7 9 10 8 6 4 2

Set in Palatino

Corgi Yearling Books are published by Random House Children's Publishers UK
61–63 Uxbridge Road, London W5 5SA

www.**kids**at**randomhouse**.co.uk
www.**randomhouse**.co.uk
www.**totallyrandombooks**.co.uk

Addresses for companies within The Random House Group Limited
can be found at: www.**randomhouse**.co.uk/offices.htm

THE RANDOM HOUSE GROUP Limited Reg. No. 954009

A CIP catalogue record for this book is available
from the British Library.

Printed and bound in the UK by CPI Group (UK) Ltd, Croydon CR0 4YY

There are no deaths in this story. Well, except for my dad, but that was over a year ago. Oh, and Dead Glyn, whose farmland started the whole thing off. No real live dead bodies, anyway.

A tower of cake, on the other hand? Yes. Forty-seven half-washed dogs, a secret plastic-coconut thrower and a hula-hooping granny? You bet! Why wouldn't there be? Every good story has a hula-hooping granny, right?

Oh, and world records. There's a whole lot of world records.

It all started with my list . . .

Monday
Chapter One

The oldest person ever to have lived, in the history of the whole world, was Jeanne Calment, a French woman, who was 122 years and 164 days old, which was pretty old considering she'd eaten whatever she wanted and smoked as many cigarettes as she wanted every day of her life to get there. Mum said I wasn't to copy that – the smoking part anyway. She died in 1997 – the French woman, not my mum – and still no one has lived long enough to beat her record. I figured that being the world's oldest person wouldn't be a bad record to hold, so I added it to my list. It was my birthday and I was ten, so I was already part way there.

This is what my list looked like:

RECORDS TO HOLD BY THE TIME I'M OLDER
BY LUKE S. MELDRUM

1. First Person from Jersey to Travel to the International Space Station. (I was realistic enough to know that travelling all the way to the moon might be pushing it.)

2. Winner of the Fastest Wheelbarrow Race. Current

record: 14.87 seconds to cover 50 metres. (The downside was I'd need a new partner, because whenever we did wheelbarrow races in PE, I was always lumbered with Martin, who had asthma and weak wrists, and had to keep stopping every three seconds.)

3. Squirting Milk from the Eye for the Furthest Distance. (I was pretty A-OK at this, except I had to practise when Mum was out and then secretly fill up the milk bottle with water because Mum thought squirting milk from my eye – or squirting anything from my eye, for that matter – was disgusting.)

4. Fastest Cup Stacker. Three cups stacked into three pyramids, three times. Current record: 5.93 seconds.

It was a work in progress, and I knew I'd have to wait a while before I could break the world's oldest person record. 112 years and 165 days, actually. But I reckoned I'd do it. On the very day I was born – 25th July 2001 – a village in France broke the record for the most people in a conga line, so luck was on my side.

As I added to my list, Mum shouted up the stairs for me. She was worried that I was too short for my age, so every birthday, after giving me my presents, she made me stand against the kitchen wall while she measured how much I'd grown. And every year Grandad Barry always laughed and said, 'If you don't grow, we'll have to put you on the rack and stretch you,' which I didn't find particularly funny.

That was exactly the sort of thing they used to do in medieval times, and I bet no one who'd had their bones stretched had ever laughed about it.

So for a few weeks before my birthday I had been doing my secret reaching exercises before bed, where I tried to reach up to the top bookshelf in my bedroom and grab any one of my record books from 1971–1992 to make myself taller. I'd borrowed a yoga book from the library and followed the instruction to *Stand on the balls of your feet, and extend your chest through your side ribs.* Except I secretly didn't mind if I didn't grab any of my record books from 1971–1992 because they were the ones without the glow-in-the-dark pictures, and weren't as interesting as the rest.

But the thought of presents more than made up for all the medieval-rack jokes, so I ran down the stairs as fast as my still-growing legs would take me.

Mum was waiting by the vegetable patch in the garden in her faded jeans, wellies and T-shirt. All button-less, naturally, what with her phobia and everything. 'Happy birthday, love,' Mum said, and held out a present. I tore open the wrapping paper and saw the latest world records DVD game. It was the one where you could play against the clock and guess who broke which record. I loved those DVDs, because the one thing to know about me is that I know *everything* there is to know about world records. I've got a near-photographic memory, see, so I remember pretty much everything, and I *always* get all the DVD questions right. Well, almost always. Last year, I'd made the mistake of naming the reticulated python as the world's longest venomous snake, when everyone knows it's the king cobra. In my defence, I hadn't been paying that much attention because Mum had just given me a bowl of chocolate ice cream when that question came on.

'Brilliant,' I said to Mum. 'I wanted this one.'

'Really?' she laughed. 'It's all you've talked about for the last two months.'

On the back of the DVD was a picture of Vinnie Denton, who was just about the coolest person in the world. As an adjudicator, he travelled all over the world and confirmed whether people had broken a record or not once they'd attempted it. Vinnie Denton was friends with the World's Hairiest Man, and with the Woman with the Most Tattoos, and with people who swallow swords for fun, but Mum said I wasn't to copy that, either.

Then a few of the old ladies who lived in the village stopped by the garden wall and gave me a sponge cake. 'Happy birthday, Luke,' one woman said, and ruffled my hair. Not that you'd notice – Mum said my hair always looked ruffled and unruly.

Mum gave Gwyn, the lady with the Victoria sponge, a Look of Thunder when she gave me the cake. It was the same look she gave me when I said something I shouldn't have in front of other people. Like the time Mum had said to her friend Jackie that she looked like she'd lost loads of weight on her diet and I'd said, 'That wasn't what you said in the car, Mum,' because Mum had told a fib. Mum had had to force a laugh, whilst Jackie looked like she was going to cry. She had a whole list of Looks, did Mum, but the thunder one was her worst.

'*I'm* making him a cake, you know,' Mum said, in a tone that implied she wasn't impressed by Gwyn's act of generosity. I decided not to say anything, because Mum's cakes were pretty awful, actually, and secretly I was pleased someone had brought me a backup. In fact, *nobody* said anything at that point, and it was clear that everyone was thinking the same thing. Mum's baking was a bit of a talking point in Port Bren, see.

Then Michael walked up the garden path and Mum got a soppy *Isn't he wonderful?* look on her face, which is what she always did when Michael was around, because she thought he was Jersey's answer to George Clooney. I didn't mind the look this time though, because as Michael walked towards me, he wheeled a brand-new BMX bike, which was silver all over. It. Was. Brilliant.

'Wow!' I shouted as I jumped off the garden wall in delight. 'Thanks!'

'Oh, you shouldn't have,' Mum said to Michael. He slung his arm round her and shrugged as if it was nothing. It *was* nothing – Michael could afford to buy the whole bike shop if he wanted.

Mum looked at me, and then nodded her head towards Michael. 'Well, thank him then,' she said.

'I did,' I replied.

'Properly,' Mum warned, and she motioned for me to hug him. I hung back a second because I thought hugging was really soppy, but Mum looked like she was forming one of her *Just do it* looks.

I shuffled over to Michael, held out my arm and gave him a quick squeeze. Michael patted my hand. 'You're welcome,' he said.

It was all a bit awkward really, so I jumped on the BMX as quickly as I could.

I was about to start riding round the garden when Mum blocked my path. 'Where's your helmet?' she asked.

'He'll be fine,' Michael said.

Mum shot Michael a *Don't start* look and went back inside the house, just as Grandad Barry was coming out of it. 'Oops,' Grandad Barry said as he tried not to barge into her, 'it's like market day in Cairo here.' Grandad Barry always found it hard not to barge into people if he got too close to them, because his belly was huge and stuck out a bit of a way in front of him. It made him look like he'd shoved a pillow up his top. Mum was forever putting him on a diet.

'What's all the racket about?' Grandad Barry yawned, scratching at his special-occasion toupee (birthdays). He pulled his dressing gown tighter around him, but it was either a size too small, or Grandad Barry's belly had expanded since he'd bought it, because his gold ceremonial chains were clearly on display.

'I've told you not to wear those things to bed,' Mum chided as the chains glinted in the morning sun.

Grandad Barry stuttered as he put his hand to his neck in an attempt to cover them. 'I didn't – I was just trying them on . . .'

Mum waggled a finger at him. 'The gold keeps rubbing off on the sheets.'

Michael tried to hide a snort, but he was pretty rubbish at it. 'That's what happens when you buy cheap gold,' he laughed.

Grandad Barry looked sheepish, but stroked the chains fondly. 'They've done me well for my entire history in office, thank you very much. Elected Mayor of Port Bren for the last nineteen years in a row. Except for that unpleasant business in 'ninety-four, but we don't talk about that.'

Grandad Barry passed me a small parcel. 'It's not much, mind,' he said as I tore it open in delight. It was a dictionary. *Who gets someone a dictionary for a present?* 'But you like your facts, don't you? And I know you like reading.' I *loved* reading, actually, but normally something to do with world records. Or at the very least, something with a bit of a story to it.

Michael tried to cover up a snort again. 'It's hardly a page-turner,' he laughed.

I frowned. 'Thanks, Grandad,' I replied. 'It's the best gift ever.'

It was OK to say this, because it was a White Lie, and after the whole Jackie-Weight-Loss incident, Mum had said that White Lies were OK sometimes, if they spared someone's feelings. Michael looked a little surprised by my comment, what with having just splashed out on a BMX, but I didn't care. Nobody insults my grandad.

Mum returned and held out my helmet. 'No buts!' she said before I could even say anything. I strapped it under my chin without protesting, because when Mum said 'No buts!' she meant it and there was no point in trying to argue otherwise. Especially when it came to safety.

'I'll go and see Dad now, I think,' I said after a while. I

put the world records DVD into my pocket and rode off up the lane.

It was easy for me to see Dad whenever I wanted as he was always in the same place – the graveyard in Port Bren, the small village in Jersey where we lived. 'The shoulder', Dad had always called it, as Port Bren was a small bit of land that jutted out and away from the main island of Jersey. Surrounded by both farmland and the harbour, it was a self-contained community. 'One of the strongest parts of the body,' Dad said, and he would know – he'd tried to be the world's strongest man when he was alive.

As much as I'd rather have Dad alive and living with me, I knew at least he was only a little way away from our house. Martin, with the weak wrists, hadn't seen his dad since he was three, because he now lived in South America with another man called Paulo. I rode like the wind and reached the church in next to no time.

This is what my dad's gravestone said:

SCOTT MELDRUM, BELOVED HUSBAND AND FATHER, BORN 1972, DIED 2010.

The gravestone always looked nice and tidy, because Mum came over and cleaned it once a month, wiping bits of grass and bird poo off it.

I talked to Dad about the sponge cake and the world records DVD, and then I showed him the BMX. I felt a little

11

guilty showing it to him, what with Michael being Mum's boyfriend now. Some ladies in the village gossiped that Mum dating Michael was too soon, but he made Mum laugh again, and I was glad because after Dad died Mum didn't laugh for ages. And he bought me presents all the time, occasionally for no reason, so that was nice. But Gwyn had said Dad 'wasn't even cold in the ground' when Michael asked Mum out and that worried me slightly. Should we have put a blanket in with him?

'It's pretty cool, don't you think?' I said to Dad about the BMX. I didn't mention the dictionary.

Then I heard a noise behind me. It was the sound of a skateboard trundling over the graveyard path, and I knew I was no longer alone. I spun round on my bike to see Tim in front of me. He flipped up his skateboard and fiddled with his earring. It was one of those earrings that made a hole in his ear lobe and pushed it open until the hole got bigger and bigger. It was disgusting. He always wore black too because he wanted to be in a death metal band. Typical. Owen and Izzy were with Tim – his little groupies. Izzy was all right at times, but Owen just did whatever Tim said. I don't know why – Owen was stocky enough to take Tim on any day of the week.

Tim motioned to my bike. 'Nice wheels,' he said in a really sarcastic way. 'The colour sucks, though. It suits you.'

Quite frankly, I was used to this sort of exchange. Tim had picked on me for as long as I could remember. And only me. Not Martin, with the weak wrists, or Victoria, in my class, who was stockier than Owen. Just me. And it had got worse since Dad had died.

'What d'you want, Tim?' I asked, because I just wanted him to get on with it. I knew what was coming. In one swift move, Tim grabbed me by the arm and yanked me off my bike. I tried to struggle free, but at thirteen, Tim was bigger and stronger than me, and his grip was watertight. He grabbed my ear and I yelped in pain as he shoved my face underneath his armpit, forcing me into a headlock. It wouldn't have been *so* bad, I thought as I gasped for breath, if Tim had bothered to use deodorant.

'Not been taking self-defence lessons from your dad, then, no?' Tim hissed in my ear, pinning one of my arms behind my back. 'Oh, wait, you can't. He's dead.'

I looked up and locked eyes with Izzy. She looked a little uneasy with it all, hopping from one foot to the other. 'C'mon, Tim,' she said and tugged at Tim's arm. 'Let's go.'

Tim shook her off. 'Shut up, Izzy,' he snapped at her. 'The little genius has gotta get used to this, 'cos when he starts our school in September . . .'

I'd planned on enjoying the summer holidays as much as I could because as sure as eggs is eggs, when I went to his

13

secondary school in September Tim would be doing this all the time. I was dreading it.

But what made everything a million times worse was that Michael was Tim's uncle. *Urgh*. Mum's new boyfriend related to my Worst Enemy. If I was being totally honest, if Mum was going to date anyone after Dad, I'd have preferred it to be someone without the nephew-from-hell.

Tim yanked my arm so hard I thought it was going to come out of its socket. My eyes watered at the pain, but I couldn't let Tim see me cry.

'Wait,' Owen yelled, 'he's trying to say something.'

'What?' Tim smirked at me. 'What is it?'

I turned my head to the side, opened my mouth to speak, then—

CRASH!! An almighty sound rumbled across the graveyard. I'd never heard anything like it.

Tim let go of me in surprise. 'What was that?' he demanded. As he looked around the graveyard, I seized the opportunity to escape and twisted out of Tim's reach. Panting heavily, I jumped on my BMX and didn't stop to look back as I sped away.

I followed the sound of the noise. There it was again, booming across the entire village. It sounded like the rumble of thunder, but there wasn't a cloud in the sky. As I rode out of the graveyard I saw a crowd of people gathered at the edge of the farmland opposite the church.

I dumped my BMX on the ground and elbowed my way through the crowd. As I got to the front, a bulldozer drove over the land. In one swift move, the driver pulled a lever and manoeuvred the bulldozer forward, its metal scooper snapping away like jaws. With the flick of another lever, a steel demolition ball smashed into the side of the farmhouse.

'What's going on?' I asked, still trying to get my breath back.

Grandad Barry, Mum and Michael joined me, and they were just as puzzled as I was. 'That's what I'd like to know,' Michael said as he stared at the half-destroyed farmhouse. 'That's my dad's land.'

Grandad Barry did a little cross in front of himself and said, 'God rest his soul,' because Michael's dad had died six months earlier, and Grandad Barry always said you shouldn't speak ill of the dead.

Jimmy, a boy in my class, hovered behind me. He took off his glasses and wiped them as if he couldn't believe what he was seeing. He was out of breath too, but not because he'd run away from Tim. Jimmy was always a bit out of breath because he was fatter than most boys.

Mum pointed to the bulldozer, and everyone saw that it was hoisting the demolition ball up in the air again. It swung once more, and she placed an arm round me to shield me from the debris. Villagers jumped back in shock and scattered out of its path. 'Watch out!' Mum cried as the remains of the farmhouse came crashing to the ground.

Chapter Two

Mr Pringle-Bliss stood on the steps of the village hall by the back of the church, his beady eyes darting from side to side as he took in the crowd. He had the misfortune of having a bulbous nose, and on top of that he was suffering from a cold, which caused his nose to balloon even further. Mr Pringle-Bliss licked his lips nervously as he stood there, and by now the whole village had gathered to find out what was going on.

'We're baying for blood,' Grandad Barry said to me. I hoped not, because I was a little squeamish when it came to blood. I once fainted when Dad accidentally sliced the top of his finger with a can-opener.

'Please,' Mr Pringle-Bliss squeaked nervously from the top step. 'Quieten down. Quieten down.' From where I stood near the front of the steps I could see him gulp. 'The council have appointed me official spokesperson.' Mr Pringle-Bliss's voice sounded a little higher than usual. 'And I have to tell you that there are to be some changes in Port Bren.'

Villagers whispered to each other in surprise. 'What changes?'

Mr Pringle-Bliss blew into a handkerchief. 'Now, bear in mind this is a good thing,' he said through his sniffles. 'It will generate income.'

The crowd started up again. 'Income?' *What was he talking about?*

Mr Pringle-Bliss winced and took another deep breath, clearly nervous about what he had to say. 'Port Bren is—' He paused to blow his nose again.

Grandad Barry threw up his arms in despair. 'Spit it out, man.'

I hoped Mr Pringle-Bliss wouldn't spit it out – I didn't fancy a face full of snot, thank you very much.

'Port Bren is to house a waste-incinerator plant,' Mr Pringle-Bliss said after a long pause.

No one said anything for a moment as his words sank in. And then everyone started talking at once. 'Waste?' they all cried.

Mr Pringle-Bliss raised his arms to silence the crowd. 'Think of the trade it'll bring,' he protested.

'Think of the pollution!' Mum shouted back at him. 'How is this a good thing?'

'We get enough trade from people coming from the mainland into the harbour,' someone piped up, and I ducked as spit flew through the air. 'We don't need waste.'

Mr Pringle-Bliss shook his head ruefully. 'It's simply not enough,' he replied. 'Not in the current climate. And tourism's not what it was.'

Next to me, Grandad Barry was standing in a state of shock, his face growing redder by the second. 'Why haven't I been told about this?' he thundered.

Mr Pringle-Bliss shrugged his shoulders weakly. 'The information has been classified up until now. On a need-to-know-only basis.'

'But I'm the Mayor!' Grandad Barry cried, spluttering in outrage. 'Not just your average civilian!'

'What's going on?' I asked. I didn't know what a waste plant was.

Grandad Barry wiped the sweat from under his toupee. 'All the rubbish that people use from the UK will be brought here and burned in a giant oven,' he replied.

Well, that didn't sound good.

The crowd roared their disapproval and Grandad Barry shouted to make himself heard over the din. 'Will we all have to move?'

'No, no. Of course not,' Mr Pringle-Bliss replied. 'We can coexist with the plant in the village' – he licked his lips nervously again – 'though some of you *will* have to move,' he mumbled under his breath.

19

Everyone was too busy yelling to notice that bit. But I was very good at hearing. Grandad Barry called me 'Bat Ears' because I always heard things I wasn't supposed to. Once, Dad had bought a work friend round to the house for drinks and, from the top of the stairs, I'd overheard Mum whisper to Grandad Barry in the front room, 'That man stinks of fish.' At least, I *thought* my excellent hearing was why Grandad Barry called me 'Bat Ears', and not because of the fact that my ears stuck out quite a bit from the side of my head – which was another thing Tim loved to tease me about.

I put up my hand to ask Mr Pringle-Bliss to repeat what he'd said, but then remembered that I wasn't at school and this was one of those situations Grandad Barry called a 'free-for-all', so I put my hand down again. 'What did you say?' I asked. '"Some of you will have to" what?'

Mr Pringle-Bliss gulped again. 'The waste plant will mostly cover this farmland,' he explained, and he motioned to the patch we were all standing on. 'We couldn't have gone ahead without its sale. But the few houses in the area around the plant will have to be demolished.'

It took me a moment to realize what he meant. *Our* house was in the area around the plant. 'That's us!' I shouted to Mum.

Mum nodded, a look of utter disbelief etched onto her

20

face. She rounded on Michael. 'Did you know about this?' she asked him forcibly. It was, after all, his dad's land.

The rest of the villagers quietened to hear him out.

Michael shook his head. 'No,' he replied firmly. 'I swear!' He held up his hands in protest and looked genuinely hurt that Mum could ever suggest such a thing.

Gwyn, the lady with the Victoria sponge, reached out and patted Michael's hand. 'It's all right, love,' she soothed. 'Fancy your dad doing a thing like this.'

He smiled gratefully at Gwyn, and Mum softened. 'I know,' Michael whispered, and he blinked like he was trying not to cry. A few of the villagers patted his back in support, and then everyone turned back to Mr Pringle-Bliss again.

'You *will* be compensated for the loss,' Mr Pringle-Bliss battled on. 'There'll be plenty of money.' He smiled weakly. 'And the plant will have a funky design, so I'm told.'

A couple of villagers whispered excitedly to each other. '*Funky*, you say?' they asked in delight. Mum glared at them.

'Are you going to take the money?' I asked Grandad Barry.

Grandad Barry cocked his head to one side to give it some thought. 'The money would be nice—' he started.

Mum leaped in like a shot. 'Not a chance,' she said,

and she gave Grandad Barry one of her Looks of Thunder. 'We've lived in this village for years. Mum died here. Scott died here. Luke was born here. We're not moving. Right, Dad?'

Grandad Barry didn't say anything. He looked like he was still thinking about the money. We'd never really had much, see.

'Dad?' Mum repeated.

Eventually Grandad Barry nodded. 'Right,' he replied, and he sounded like he meant it. He turned to Mr Pringle-Bliss. 'Don't we get a say in any of this?'

Mr Pringle-Bliss took a wad of paper from his jacket pocket. 'I was just coming to that,' he said, looking through his notes. 'The council has said that the plant can be contested—'

Mum butted in, which I thought was a bit rich, seeing as she always told me off for doing that. 'That's what we're doing now!' she cried. The rest of the villagers hooted in support.

Mr Pringle-Bliss battled on amidst the uproar. 'If we can prove the land has historic value—'

Mum butted in again. I didn't think now was the time to say anything to her. 'Of course it has,' she cried. 'It's *our* land!'

Mr Pringle-Bliss blew heavily into his handkerchief.

'Will you let me finish?' He took a deep breath and scanned his notes. '*If,*' he continued, 'within one week, we can prove that this land, and this village, has "significant historical value", then we can contest the plant on those grounds.'

'What does that mean?' Gwyn asked.

Mr Pringle-Bliss looked at the crowd of villagers in front of him and his eyes welled up with tears. 'It means that if we want to save Port Bren,' he said with sadness in his voice, 'we need to do something to get it on the map.'

Chapter Three

Less than an hour later, Mum handed round plates of cake as everyone crowded into our front room. As Mayor, Grandad Barry had taken it upon himself to assemble the entire village for an emergency meeting, so it was rammed and noisy. The sofa and armchairs had been taken by the older ladies, Mum had found a couple of beanbags in the loft and Grandad Barry had accidentally whacked Jimmy's dad over the head with a deckchair he'd brought in from the garden. I had to sit on the stairs because there wasn't any free space, even though I was one of the smallest there. Luckily the front room had a glass-panelled wall on one side, so I could see into it perfectly. The thought of cake – even Mum's cake – made my stomach rumble and I wondered if Mum would remember the birthday tea I was meant to be having. Everyone looked so angry and upset, I didn't like to ask.

Seb, a frail-looking old man, perched on the edge of an armchair. 'Look on the bright side,' he said to his neighbour. 'It could be quite fun.'

Everyone stopped talking at that. 'Fun?' Grandad Barry boomed after a moment.

'Yes,' Seb replied. 'Best thing to happen to Port Bren in ages, all those slides and whirlpools.'

Grandad Barry frowned. 'What are you talking about? No one wants a waste plant.'

Seb looked confused. 'Waste plant? I thought he was talking about a water park!'

Grandad Barry sighed and rooted around in an old oak dresser which took up nearly one side of the front room. From a side drawer, he pulled out a huge leather-bound book. Known as the *Port Bren Bible*, it was used to record significant developments in Port Bren throughout the years and was passed from one elected mayor to the next. We'd had it nineteen years in a row – except, of course, for that unpleasant business in 'ninety-four.

Grandad Barry flicked over several pages and read to the crowd. 'Now, it says here,' he said in a commanding tone, '*Port Bren dates back to eleven thirty-two, when the first English mainlanders settled.*' Grandad Barry and the villagers mimed spitting at the word 'mainlanders', like they always did.

Glyn, who was Grandad Barry's best friend, even though he sometimes forgot who Grandad Barry was, forgot the mime part. Mum tactfully wiped saliva from her eye.

25

Grandad Barry scanned the rest of the book. 'But there's nothing to say that Port Bren has "historic value".'

Gwyn held up a small cash box. 'I've got some savings,' she said. 'We could buy the land back.'

Michael sighed. 'It's too late, Gwyn,' he said. 'My hands are tied. Dad saw to that.' He gave her a tight smile and she nodded in sympathy.

'Does anybody have any ideas to prove our historic worth?' Grandad Barry asked, panic creeping into his voice. 'We've only got till Sunday.'

The villagers started chatting amongst themselves.

'I've got a pot of jam from nineteen fifty-seven,' a plump old lady wedged firmly into a beanbag exclaimed breathlessly. 'It's not even opened.'

One of the smaller boys from my school stuck up his hand. 'I once saw a badger,' he stated proudly. 'Down by the harbour last Christmas.'

His mother shook her head at him. 'It was a dog,' she corrected.

'I've just created a golf course in my back garden,' Jimmy's dad shouted, rubbing the lump on his head.

'The golf course hasn't got any holes,' Grandad Barry replied. 'It's just your back garden.'

'What about cows?' someone in the crowd asked.

'What *about* cows?' Grandad Barry said, rolling his eyes.

'Every part of the UK has cows. Not just Jersey. And not just Port Bren.' He looked to see who had spoken and glared when he realized it was The Other Barry. The Other Barry was the exact opposite of Grandad Barry – fit, good for his age and with a full head of hair. 'Might have known,' Grandad Barry muttered under his breath.

Just then, Glyn piped up. 'Hang on, old bean,' he shouted. 'The Queen once visited Port Bren! In nineteen sixty-eight. That's historic, isn't it?'

Everyone in the crowd gasped in surprise. 'She did?' Grandad Barry asked, his snowy-white eyebrows raised heavenwards. 'I don't remember that. Mind you, I wasn't Mayor then.' He flicked through the *Port Bren Bible*. 'Nineteen sixty-eight, you say? There's no record of it.'

Glyn scratched his head in confusion. 'Oh – oh – wait a second,' he said. 'Nope, it wasn't the Queen. I remember now. It was my cousin, Beardy Jim. I always get those two mixed up.'

The villagers let out a collective sigh of disappointment, but Grandad Barry snapped the book shut, determined not to be defeated. 'If we can't prove this village already has value,' he said, 'then we need to do something to make us famous. That's what Mr Pringle-Bliss said. *Get us on the map*. That's the only way we can stop the plant.'

The Other Barry stuck his hand in the air. 'I went up in a

hot-air balloon once,' he said. 'That was pretty historic.'

'For you, maybe,' Grandad Barry replied between gritted teeth. 'For us, it's barely an anecdote. And we've moved on from being "historic". We're on being famous now.'

Mum gestured to the computer screen at the back of the room, where she played an Internet video of a crowd of people throwing tomatoes at each other. '*La Tomatina*,' she said.

Grandad Barry sighed and rubbed his temples. He looked like he was struggling to keep his cool. 'Yes, thank you for the French, Mary,' he said to her sarcastically, 'but we're trying to think of ways to save our homes.'

Mum shrugged, used to Grandad Barry's sarcasm. 'It's a festival in Spain,' she replied calmly. 'Thousands and thousands of people go to this little village every year and throw tomatoes at each other. It's tradition.'

Everyone looked strangely at her, after hearing her crazy fact.

Grandad Barry spoke slowly. 'R-i-i-i-ght,' he replied, unconvinced. 'Nice idea, but we'd never get those sorts of numbers. We're hardly the Jersey Battle of Flowers, are we? Thousands of people in Port Bren throwing food at each other? Never in a million years. Two hundred-odd people live in Port Bren, not two thousand.' He choked slightly on the piece of cake he was eating and gave Mum a funny look. 'Some of them *very* odd. What have you put in this one?'

'Couscous and balsamic vinegar,' Mum replied. 'I thought I'd go exotic this time.'

That was the thing about her cakes. Mum was always 'going exotic' with them. I don't know why – her spag bol and her Sunday roasts were the best in Port Bren, but for some reason Mum always wanted to 'go exotic' when it came to cakes.

Grandad Barry put down the cake and shrugged to his neighbour. 'Great,' he whispered, and I really had to strain to hear what he said. 'We're going to be known for waste *and* her God-awful cakes.' Everyone waited until Mum wasn't looking and then tossed their cake into a plant pot.

'She's no Mr Kipling,' Gwyn whispered conspiratorially to Glyn.

He looked confused. 'Is that the new vicar?' he asked.

I didn't feel like listening to much more after that, because nobody had had a sensible idea about how to save the village for ages. In fact, nobody had had a sensible idea at all. I walked up the stairs and headed back to my bedroom.

It was my favourite room in the house. Mum had let me put up posters of famous record breakers on the wall. There was Robert Wadlow, who was the tallest man ever recorded, measuring 2.72 metres, the same height as a lorry. I always wondered how many secret reaching exercises I'd have to do to grow as tall as that. Next to Mr Wadlow was He Pingping from China who, at 74 centimetres, was once the world's smallest man. I liked the contrast of putting the tallest man and the smallest man next to each other; plus, the smallest man always made me feel a little better about my own height. I'd have bet anything that He Pingping would have been bullied at school too – if not for his height, then definitely for his name.

I wandered over to the fish tank on top of my chest of drawers and waved to my two goldfish, Jaws and Christopher Columbus. So named because one was always hungry and ate everything in sight; the other because, for a fish, I thought he was quite the explorer. Christopher Columbus always looked like he wanted to escape the goldfish bowl and investigate the wider world. The pond, maybe.

I sprinkled a handful of food into the tank and then sat down at my desk. I picked up my plastic cups, because number four on my list of records to hold before I was older was cup stacking. I'd practised hundreds and hundreds of times, but I wasn't quite there yet.

Grandad Barry poked his head round the door. 'All

right, son?' he asked, and nodded to Dead Glyn's farm-land opposite the house. 'Any thoughts on what we can do? You're the brains of the family.'

When he wasn't calling me 'Bat Ears', Grandad Barry called me 'The Brains', which was to do with the reason I was going to secondary school in September, a whole year earlier than most boys my age. This was another thing Tim always teased me about. Mrs Wilson, the headmistress, called me 'gifted', but I didn't receive any extra presents for it.

I shrugged my shoulders. 'Dunno,' I said. 'You'll think of something.'

'You could still email your friends,' Grandad Barry replied, 'if we do have to move.'

I didn't look up from stacking my cups. But then another thought popped into my head. 'You wouldn't move without me, would you, Grandad?' I said. 'And leave me here?

Grandad Barry started to laugh, but then he caught the worried look on my face. 'Don't be daft,' he replied. 'Whatever gave you that idea?'

People always leave, I thought to myself. Dad upping and dying out of nowhere had taught me that. But I didn't say anything.

'There are other parts of Jersey that are quite nice,' Grandad Barry said, gazing out of the window. 'Not all are so close to the sea, mind, but nice enough.'

31

I knew that Mum didn't want to leave the village, and it was the only home I'd ever known, but the more I thought about it, the more I figured that moving wouldn't be *so* bad. 'As far as I'm concerned,' I said under my breath, 'the further away from Tim we move the better.'

Grandad Barry obviously didn't have Bat Ears, because he just smiled and shut the door. I heard him pad downstairs and I was glad. I didn't want to have to tell him that I didn't have any friends to email.

Determined to do anything to stop the waste plant, the villagers had concocted a plan, of sorts. I sat on my BMX at the edge of Dead Glyn's farmland and watched from the sidelines as Mum and a band of villagers waved placards and chanted in protest.

'WHAT DO WE WANT?' Mum shouted.

'SAVE PORT BREN!' everyone yelled back.

'WHEN DO WE WANT IT?'

'NOW!'

'OR BY SUNDAY!' Walking-Stick Glyn shouted, not quite getting it.

A reporter from the *Jersey Journal* newspaper with receding ginger hair and at least fifty freckles on his face watched the protest and scribbled something on a notepad. He looked incredibly bored. 'I'm off,' he shouted to Mum over the chants.

'We're not done yet!' Mum exclaimed. 'We've written protest songs, and everything.'

The reporter sighed. 'I'm not being funny, love,' he

33

said, and scratched his chin, 'but this ain't interesting.'

Mum shot him one of her *Downright livid* looks. It used to be called *Downright angry* but I looked up 'livid' in the dictionary Grandad Barry gave me, and thought that sounded much more like it.

'Is that what the rest of the world thinks of Port Bren?' Mum asked the reporter. 'Shoved away on this tiny island, that we're only fit for waste?'

The reporter shook his head. 'No, I don't think the rest of the world thinks of you like that,' he laughed. 'I don't think the rest of the world thinks of you *at all*. That's the problem.'

Jimmy pedalled up on his bike towards me and motioned to the protestors. 'Do you think we should do something to help?' he asked.

I kicked away my bike stand. 'Nah,' I said. 'Leave them to it.'

In the distance, a car horn tooted. It was Lloyd, an old man who had more white hair growing out of his ears than on top of his head. His ear hair was so long he sometimes wore it in bunches. Lloyd drove slowly by in a flashy silver sports car, looking incredibly pleased with himself. 'I took the money, man!' he told anyone who would listen.

Mum shook her placard at him in disgust. 'What about the rest of us?' she asked, *not* incredibly pleased with *him*.

Lloyd shrugged his shoulders, not a care in the world. 'At my time of life, why not?'

'It's not going too well,' Jimmy whispered to me.

'It is for Lloyd,' I replied. I pedalled across the fields because I couldn't see where this was going.

A wheezing sound behind me told me Jimmy was racing to catch up. 'I wonder what they'll do with all the bodies,' he said in between breaths.

'What?' I asked. I didn't have a clue what he was going on about.

Jimmy motioned to the church behind him. 'When they tear up the graveyard,' he replied.

I stopped in my tracks. *Tear up the graveyard?*

Jimmy must have seen how confused I was because he carried on. 'My dad saw the plans,' he explained. 'To build the plant, seven houses – including yours – and the grave-yard have to go.'

Well, that was all too much.

I burst to the front of the crowd on the farmland. 'They're tearing up the graveyard!' I cried. Mum and Grandad Barry exchanged a look and then Mum put her arm round me. 'We're not going to let that happen,' she said.

I didn't know what to say. I tried to protest, but I couldn't get the words out. 'They can't!' I panicked. *What would they do to Dad? What would they do with his body? Where*

would Mum go to keep his grave nice and tidy and give it a clean once a month to get rid of all the bits of grass and bird poo?

Mum squeezed my shoulder. 'We'll get the newspapers involved,' she explained, and gave the reporter another of her *Downright livid* looks. '*Real* papers. Someone will pay attention. I promise.'

I wasn't convinced because their protest hadn't seemed to work so far. All I knew was that I had to do something. I couldn't let the plant be built. I couldn't let the plant tear the graveyard to pieces and dig up Dad. And a few home-made chants and placards were *not* going to do it.

I thought hard about how *I* could do it. Long and hard. Longer and harder than I had for my maths test in advanced mental maths last month, and I'd got twenty out of twenty for that.

Then suddenly I had an idea. And it was simply and utterly the best idea that I had ever had.

I jumped back on my BMX and rode across the fields and down the winding lane to our house. Jimmy obviously saw how fast I was going, because he didn't even try to follow me.

I burst into my bedroom and grabbed the nearest record book I could find. I didn't even care that it was from 1979 and didn't have any glow-in-the-dark pictures inside. I picked up the DVD that Mum had given me for my birthday and bundled together the plastic cups from the desk. Oh, yes, it was the best idea ever.

I juggled the cups, the record book and the DVD in my arms and elbowed my way through the crowd on the farm-land once more. 'Mum!' I yelled as I pushed my way to the front. 'Mum, I've got it! I know how we can save the village.'

Mum took one look at what I was carrying and then grabbed me squarely by the shoulders. She took me by surprise and I dropped a couple of cups. 'No,' she said. 'Absolutely not.'

'Why not?' I asked.

'You know why not,' Mum replied.

From behind her, Michael chipped in. 'I think it's a great idea,' he said. *Well done, Michael*, I thought, but Mum gave him one of her Looks.

I couldn't wait any longer. This was too important. 'But, Mum,' I said. 'It's not a dangerous one.' I had to say this because I knew how Mum felt about record attempts – and about dangerous record attempts in particular, what with how Dad died and everything. I held out my cups to her. 'It's cup stacking.'

Mum didn't say anything for the longest time and I had no idea what she was thinking. She didn't frown or smile or do anything.

In the distance, the sound of a digger bellowed out as it revved into action. The sound travelled across the farmland and I seized the opportunity. It was such a perfect plan; I knew there was no way this could fail. 'What else are we going to do to save the village?' I asked.

Mum opened her mouth to speak, but I jumped in before she could reply. 'I'll call them,' I said. 'They'll send someone to adjudicate. You know, to make it official.'

I held up the DVD and pointed to Vinnie Denton's grinning face on the back. 'And I know just the man for the job,' I said.

Wednesday
Chapter Five

The next day, after I'd practised my cup stacking over and over again, the village of Port Bren got ready for my world-record attempt. The adjudicating headquarters had had a last-minute cancellation so Vinnie Denton could fit me in right away. Luckily nothing much happened in Port Bren – and certainly nothing as momentous as this – so, despite the short notice, everyone was free to help out.

And Port Bren went crazy.

The village green had been decorated as if it was the August Bank Holiday Summer Fair, though that wasn't for another month yet. Stalls were set up everywhere. There was a tombola, a coconut shy, a yellow bouncy castle in the shape of a medieval fortress, and Mrs Wilson, the head-mistress, had strung up bunting all around. The only trouble was, what with the short notice, she'd only managed to find the national-flag-of-Ghana banners we last used for World Culture Day. But they looked nice and bright, which was the main thing.

Vinnie Denton was meant to arrive at four p.m. I checked

my watch – it was quarter-past. I knew Vinnie Denton would be travelling from London, by ferry and by car, so there was every chance the boat could have been late. But it was all setting my nerves on edge; my stomach felt like it was tied into one big knot and I'd had to go to the loo at least three times in the last half-hour.

After what felt like an eternity, the sound of an approaching car echoed down the lane. All the villagers stopped what they were doing and rushed forward to meet it. *This was it!* A small brass band played by the roadside – so small that it consisted of just Cheryl, the baker, on triangle, Roy Fort, the butcher, on a tin trumpet, and his son blowing one of those party blowers you get for birthdays and New Year. I wasn't sure, but it sounded a bit like 'Jingle Bells'.

I couldn't wait any longer – I was more excited about meeting Vinnie Denton than I would have been if it was Christmas morning and I'd just seen my first snowflake. Vinnie Denton, the coolest man ever. Vinnie Denton, who had travelled far and wide. Vinnie Denton, who could make me a record breaker.

I ran forward in eager anticipation, about to burst with joy as Vinnie Denton got out of the car.

Except it wasn't Vinnie Denton.

A tall, thin man with short brown hair that stuck up in

several places it probably wasn't meant to climbed from the clapped-out car instead. He carried a briefcase in one hand and a glass case in the other. The man straightened his tie, tried to smooth down his hair and started walking towards us.

'You're not the guy from the DVD,' I said, when he eventually reached me.

'No, I'm not,' the man replied. 'I'm Simon David.' He juggled his briefcase and the glass case so he could offer his hand to me.

'I wanted the guy from the DVD,' I said. 'Vinnie Denton.'

Simon sighed. 'People always do.' A sad smile flickered across his face. 'And why wouldn't they? Vinnie's *always* on the DVDs. He makes friends with record breakers wherever he goes.'

I rolled my eyes – that was *exactly* why I wanted him.

'And he's never had a panic attack over heights in his life,' Simon added.

I wasn't sure what to make of this. 'Uh, good for him,' I said. I studied Simon David closely. He certainly looked like an adjudicator, all smart suit, briefcase and clipboard. But as he stood on the edge of the green, his hand outstretched to shake mine, I had a million questions for him. First, where was Vinnie Denton? Second, why did Simon David have two first names?

41

'Bit of a mix-up at head office,' Simon muttered, interrupting my thoughts. 'It's just me, I'm afraid.'

Still, I reasoned above anything else, one world-record adjudicator was better than no world-record adjudicator. I took Simon's hand and shook it with gusto. 'You'll do,' I said.

Simon smiled, and we walked towards the green where everyone was waiting. 'I have, like, every book about records ever,' I said, to show that I really knew what I was talking about. 'I've read them all about a million times. How brilliant is it going to be to break this record!'

Simon stopped in his tracks. '*You're* the competitor?' he asked, scanning his clipboard. I nodded, and Simon started walking again, but so quickly that I had to run to catch up.

'I'm sorry,' Simon explained. 'I can't spend too much time with you before the attempt. Might be frowned upon, you see.'

I walked on beside him regardless and peered into the glass case Simon carried under his other arm. Inside it was a tarantula. A massive, hairy tarantula curled up in one corner, sleeping on a bed of moss and twigs. I'd never seen one up close before, though I knew all about the involvement of tarantulas in world records. The most soap bubbles blown whilst having a tarantula in your mouth, for example, was 119 in thirty seconds. 'Wow!' I said. 'Cool spider. I really want a gecko, but Grandad's not sure. Says they wee everywhere.' I leaned in to take a closer look.

'His name is Sir Walter,' Simon explained, clearly forgetting he wasn't meant to be talking to me. 'After Sir Walter Raleigh, the explorer' – he paused to think for a second – 'kind of appropriate, isn't it?' he said. 'What with the real Sir Walter having once been Governor of Jersey.'

I looked up in surprise. 'I didn't know that!'

Simon smiled. 'Useless facts. I'm full of them.' He tapped the glass and the spider twitched one of its legs but remained asleep. 'He used to be a bit more active in his younger days,' Simon laughed. 'He always looked like he wanted to explore the wider world. Now he doesn't care if we're in Honolulu or Hampshire.'

I couldn't believe it. Sir Walter was just like Christopher Columbus! Except the not-being-a-fish part.

Grandad Barry slapped Simon heartily on the back as he reached the green. 'Barry's the name,' he boomed. 'Elected Mayor of Port Bren nineteen years in a row. Except for that unpleasant business in 'ninety-four, but we don't talk about that.' He frowned at Simon. 'Mainland, are you? Well, can't have everything.' Grandad Barry didn't spit when he said 'mainland' this time, as he didn't want to ruin my chances. So he frowned a lot at Simon instead. I never really quite understood what the older Port Bren residents had against mainlanders, and, secretly, I think even Grandad Barry had forgotten.

Grandad Barry manoeuvred Simon towards the coconut shy that Mum was helping to run. 'My daughter, Mary,' he said. Simon did a little double take, which is what a lot of men do when they meet Mum because she's very beautiful. I never knew my granny, but she was Irish, and Grandad Barry said Mum took after her. 'All eyes as green as emeralds and red rosy cheeks,' he told me. 'And the temper that flares up with no warning.' That I had seen.

Grandad Barry nudged Simon forward to the coconut stall. 'Don't be shy,' he boomed, and laughed at his joke.

Mum rolled her eyes and extended her hand to Simon. He went to shake it, but he didn't see that it contained a glass of punch. The drink spilled everywhere.

'Oh! Oh, I'm so sorry,' Simon said and he panicked a little as he tried to mop it up with his tie.

Mum wiped her hands on her dress. 'It's fine,' she said. 'Just leave it.' But I could tell from her voice that it was definitely *not* fine.

Simon must have heard it too, because he said, 'Sorry. The same thing happened in Monkey's Eyebrow last week.'

'What?' Mum asked warily.

'It's in Arizona,' Simon replied. 'No one ever knows those things.'

Grandad Barry took his arm, led him away from the madness and pointed to a parade of people. 'This is The Other Barry, Gwyn, Glyn, Bryn and—'

'Flynn?' Simon interrupted. He laughed, amused at his own joke.

'Dave,' Grandad Barry replied with a frown.

I was too busy being nervous to laugh at that. I'd half a mind to cancel the cup stacking and go for some sort of sweat-based record instead. Most beads of sweat on forehead, perhaps?

Then I sensed someone hovering beside me. 'How are you feeling?' Simon asked, smiling down on me.

I shrugged my shoulders, my mouth too dry to talk.

Simon coughed and straightened his tie. 'Well, if you'd prefer we got on with it—'

'Ashrita Furman says you should always think of everything that could go wrong' – I quickly interrupted him – 'and then prepare for all eventualities.' Simon laughed. 'What?' I asked. 'Ashrita should know – he's the person with the most world records broken ever.'

'One hundred records and still going strong.' Simon beamed and looked at me in admiration. 'You certainly know your stuff.' He squatted down a bit so his face was level with mine. 'But he also said that if your record attempt doesn't make you happy, then you shouldn't

45

do it. Having fun is a big part of breaking a record.'

I didn't say anything. Saving Dad was more important than having fun.

Simon nodded that it was time to start the record attempt, so I took a few deep breaths and stood behind a table in the centre of the green. I put my cups on the table and felt the eyes of the entire village on me. Even Mum, who didn't want me doing it, looked on, though she lurked at the back.

Simon positioned himself to one side of the table holding his clipboard and stopwatch. 'I'm looking for three repetitions of the pyramid to complete the attempt,' he said to me. 'You're looking to beat five point nine three seconds to break the record. Understood?'

I nodded and wiped the sweat off my hands.

At the front of the crowd, the *Jersey Journal* reporter whispered to his neighbour. 'You're resting the hopes of your village on a kid with cups?' he hissed. I looked over at him – having heard with my Bat Ears – and frowned. I didn't find the comment particularly helpful.

Mum must have heard as well because she glowered at him and he blushed and turned as red as his hair.

'Ready?' Simon asked me.

I nodded, but I didn't feel it. It felt as though I had a swarm of butterflies fluttering in my tummy.

'On three,' Simon instructed. 'One . . .'

My throat was as dry as the Sahara desert.

'Two . . .'

I cracked my knuckles and ignored Mum's *Don't be disgusting* look.

'Three.'

That was it! I was off. I formed a pyramid with the nine cups and then stacked them into three piles as quickly as I could. My hands worked like the clappers. I think the village must have half expected to see steam rise from the table.

At that moment someone half coughed and half shouted at me. 'LOSER!'

The cry echoed all round the green and I faltered at the disruption. From the corner of my eye, I could see Tim and Owen snigger. Typical. Trust Tim to try and ruin everything. *Why hadn't I prepared for that eventuality?* Still, I knew I couldn't stop, so I battled on, determined. After what felt like no time at all, I'd finished. I held up my hands and stepped back from the table. 'Done!' I said.

Simon clicked the stopwatch. I could feel my heart pounding in my chest, one hundred, two hundred beats a minute. I wiped my sweaty palms on my jeans. 'Five point nine two seconds,' I whispered under my breath and clenched my fists beside me in anticipation. 'Please. Five point nine two seconds.'

Simon raised his head from the stopwatch. 'Eight point zero three seconds,' he said. 'Two point eleven seconds short.'

It took a moment for Simon's words to sink in. Time seemed to stand still.

Then the villagers all gasped as one and I knew that I'd failed. I had let down the village. I'd let down my dad. *Now what were we going to do?*

Chapter Six

I felt hot flashes of pain behind my eyes and I knew that I was going to cry. I tried to think of something happy – I didn't want to give Tim any more ammunition.

Mum came out of the crowd and stood by me. 'Not to worry, love,' she said softly, and she rubbed my back. 'You gave it your best shot. That's all anyone can ask.'

Michael turned to Simon. 'Can't you give it to him?' he called.

The villagers seemed to like that. 'Yeah,' they all shouted. 'Go on! Let him have it!'

Simon didn't say anything, but in my heart of hearts I knew he wouldn't. I had failed, and an adjudicator would never allow someone to pass just because a village full of people shouted at him to.

Simon shook his head. 'I can't,' he replied. 'An attempt in Quicksand last month was more successful.'

'What?' Michael cried, confused.

'It's in Kentucky,' I said softly, not quite able to meet Simon's gaze.

Simon peered over his clipboard at me. 'No one ever knows those things,' he said in amazement. 'Still, rules are rules, I'm afraid.'

'And rules are there to be broken!' Michael shouted.

'We need to save Port Bren!' Grandad Barry yelled. 'Don't be such a square, man!'

THWACK! From nowhere, a plastic coconut from the coconut shy smacked Simon in the head. 'Owww!' he cried.

Simon rubbed his temple and looked for the culprit. I knew it was Grandad Barry, but he simply whistled to the heavens and avoided Simon's gaze. 'Look,' Simon continued firmly. 'I can't give it to him when he didn't break the record. But if Luke wants to, he can try again.'

The villagers all turned to me in anticipation. I thought for a moment. I could give it another go . . .

But then I caught Tim's eye. He laughed and pulled faces at me behind the villagers' backs. *How could I concentrate when he was there?* I looked up to Mum, but she hadn't seen him. She was just gazing off into the distance, biting her lip.

I sighed and shook my head. 'No.'

Mum didn't say anything, but I could tell she was glad all this record business was now over. Grandad Barry ruffled my hair. 'We'll think of something else, lad,' he said.

With the attempt now over, Simon packed away his

clipboard. 'I'll be off, then,' he said, and he gave me a tight smile. 'Maybe next time, hey?'

I looked down at my feet. 'There won't be a next time,' I muttered. 'We've only got till Sunday.'

Simon looked confused but I didn't explain. He picked up Sir Walter's case and walked off the green. With that, all the villagers started to leave. Roy Fort stopped playing his tin trumpet. The coconuts fell off their stands. Nobody said anything, but I could tell that everyone was disappointed I hadn't broken the record. They'd placed their hopes of saving the village in me, and I'd let them all down. If only there *was* a next time. If only I *could* try again, without Tim's eagle eyes boring into me, willing me to fail. If only I could get Simon alone.

Simon clunked the seatbelt over Sir Walter's case as he strapped it into the passenger seat and turned the key in the ignition. Nothing happened. He tried again, but the engine just stuttered and stalled. It made a pathetic attempt at starting, gave a low moan and then finally gave up the ghost.

Simon climbed out of the car and popped open the bonnet. 'Perfect,' he muttered. 'This is all I need.'

He looked up from the engine and called out to me, Mum and Grandad Barry, the only villagers still dawdling on the green. 'Excuse me!' he shouted. 'Is there a mechanic here?'

51

'Yes,' Grandad Barry called back. 'Cumbria.'

'What?' Simon wasn't sure he'd heard properly. Cumbria was five hundred miles and a ferry ride away.

'He's on holiday,' Grandad Barry explained.

'When's he back?'

'Friday. Tell you what, Marvel Barton might have one.'

Simon perked up. 'Great. Where's that?'

'Next village over. But nobody will take you at this hour.'

'Is there a bus service to the ferry?' Simon asked.

'Oh, yes,' Grandad Barry replied proudly. 'Never let it be said that Port Bren doesn't have public transport.'

'Right. When's the next bus?'

Grandad Barry checked his watch. 'Friday.'

Simon was starting to look panicked and pulled his mobile from his pocket, shaking it vigorously. 'No signal?' Grandad Barry asked. 'No, we never did get round to installing a phone mast. And now, well, now I guess there's no point.'

I took in the scene. Simon's broken car. No mechanic in sight. Too dark to drive to the next town to find one. I decided to seize the opportunity. 'Simon could stay, just for tonight,' I suggested.

Mum shot me one of her *Not at all impressed* looks and forced a laugh. 'I'm sure Mr David has other plans.'

Simon closed the bonnet, moved round to the back of the

car and, out of sheer determination, started to push. It didn't budge. 'I've got to get to Devon,' he said, straining.

Grandad Barry looked incredulous. 'To the mainland?' he thundered and spat in outrage. 'Why on earth would you want to do that?'

The car alarm went off and, truly flustered, Simon yanked his keys from the ignition. 'Is there not a chance we could go to Marvel Barton now?' he asked as he clicked off the alarm.

Grandad Barry's laugh boomed out. 'Marvel Barton's twenty miles away, son,' he explained. 'I've only got the tractor.'

'He could stay, just for tonight,' I repeated. Grandad Barry looked from me to Simon.

'Fine,' Grandad Barry said kindly. 'We'll go to Marvel Barton tomorrow.'

I clenched my fist in delight. '*Yesssss!*' I hissed under my breath.

'I should phone my boss,' Simon said. 'Max was very, uh, insistent.' With a sigh, he and Sir Walter reluctantly followed us all home.

In the kitchen I laid the table as Mum bustled about with bowls of carrots and cauliflower. Phase one of my plan was complete: I'd managed to get Simon alone, away from Tim.

I now had to get him to give me another go at the record.

Sir Walter's case rested on the sideboard as Simon made a phone call to his boss. Simon held the phone away from his ear, but I could hear Max shouting into it on the other end. 'So, just a temporary setback, sir,' Simon stuttered when he eventually got a word in. 'No, not another panic attack. Not like Norway. Yes, Devon, tomorrow, nine o'clock. I'll definitely be there. Yes, this number if you can't get me on the mobile, if there are problems – which there won't be,' Simon added hastily. 'Thank you, sir.'

Simon hung up the phone and mopped his brow with a hanky. He hovered awkwardly to one side, not sure whether the etiquette of being an unwanted house guest meant he should at least offer to lay the table, or something.

Grandad Barry picked up on his quandary. 'There's no standing on ceremony in this house, man,' he boomed, and gestured for Simon to help.

Simon opened a kitchen cabinet and pulled out four mugs from the back. He followed me around the table and set a mug by each place mat. I've no idea why – no one was having tea.

Mum placed a sizzling roast chicken in the middle of the table and we all started piling food onto our plates. Grandad Barry tucked a napkin under his chin to protect his ceremonial gold chains from gravy stains, whilst Simon organized his plate into three sections – meat, potatoes and vegetables. He was very thorough about it. 'I don't normally do this sort of thing,' he said. 'Stay with the locals. Might be frowned upon, you see. Sorry for the inconvenience.'

Nobody replied. The general consensus between Mum and Grandad Barry was that he *was* an inconvenience.

Not me. 'Maybe Simon could help us?' I said, trying to sound as casual as I could. 'Since he's here?'

'Help with what?' Simon asked, and reached for the water jug in the middle of the table.

Grandad Barry put down his forkful of potato. 'Truth be told, son,' he said warily, 'we're on our last legs.'

'They're building a waste-incinerator plant,' Mum chipped in. 'Right here in Port Bren.'

Grandad Barry frowned at her interruption. 'Too many cooks, Mary,' he said. '*I'm* telling the story.' He turned to Simon and continued in a commanding tone. 'Now, Michael's father, Glyn, he sold his land before he died.'

'Glyn?' Simon asked. 'Wasn't he there today?'

'That's a different Glyn,' Grandad Barry replied. 'Walking-Stick Glyn. No, this is Dead Glyn, well, he sold his land and sold us right down the river, let me tell you.'

'And who's Michael?' Simon asked.

'My boyfriend,' Mum replied, levelling her gaze at him. The tips of Simon's ears started to turn red.

'Well, can't *he* do anything?' Simon asked, and poured water from the jug into his mug.

And then we all froze.

'Put that down!' I yelled as Simon lifted the mug to his lips. I hadn't meant to shout at him, it just came out.

Simon's hand froze in midair. 'What?' he whispered.

'Please put the mug down,' I said softly. We're not usually nuts about mugs, see, but this mug was special.

Simon turned the mug round and saw *World's Best Dad* written on the side. It was my dad's mug. 'Oh, is this Michael's?' he asked.

'No!' I blurted out before I knew what I was doing. 'As if!'

Mum frowned at me, but she didn't say anything. Simon opened his mouth to ask something, but Grandad Barry shook his head not to. 'You weren't to know,' Grandad Barry said. 'It's not your fault.'

Mum shot Simon one of her Looks of Thunder. 'And neither is it Michael's,' she snapped. 'Anyway, there's nothing he can do. We have to become famous on our own and contest the plant that way. That's what the council have said.'

Grandad Barry flung down his napkin theatrically. 'It's

all very well them banging on about trade and revenue, but they know as well as we do that a waste plant would bring smog and noise and chemicals. It'll tear up this community.'

I piped up again. 'You've been around the world, right, Simon?' I said. 'Adjudicating? I bet you've seen loads of places that are famous.'

Simon shook his head. 'Not really,' he replied. 'I mean, I *have* travelled practically everywhere, yes. The thing is, though,' he stumbled, avoiding everyone's gaze, 'I never get the chance to stay in one place for very long. I rarely have time to meet the locals, let alone stay with them.' He gave a tight smile. 'As much as I'd like to, frowned upon or not.'

I cleared my throat. 'I, uh, I'd like to try again,' I said. I avoided looking directly at Mum, but, from the corner of my eye, I could see her staring at me.

'Try again?' Simon repeated.

I nodded. 'With cup stacking. I bet I could do it if I didn't have so many distractions. You know, with everyone watching.'

Simon pulled at his tie. 'I don't think so.'

I looked at him in surprise. 'But you said I could try again. You said it.' I couldn't understand why he would go back on his word.

Simon patted his napkin round his mouth. He then folded it exactly in four and rested it on the table at ninety degrees to his plate. 'I meant,' he said, 'I don't think one record would be enough.'

My mind raced. 'I could try a different record!' I shouted. 'Right?' I grabbed one of my record books – 1995 – from the sideboard and flicked to various pages. 'Look: most dogs washed in an hour, furthest peanut throw . . .'

Simon shook his head. 'I'm sorry,' he said softly. 'I've never heard of only one successful attempt putting a village on the map. It wouldn't be enough to make you famous. People break records all over the world, every single day.'

Well, that didn't help the matter much. What use was it having a record adjudicator staying with us if he couldn't help save the village?

Grandad Barry gathered up the plates. 'No, I suppose not,' he sighed. 'Still, nice to think we could, while it lasted.'

And that was the end of that.

Later that evening I went to the bathroom to brush my teeth. I had to sneak quietly because I'd told Mum I'd already cleaned them when she shouted up the stairs to ask. Really, I'd been playing my world record DVD on the DVD player Michael had bought me last month.

I hid behind an old dresser on the landing as Mum came up the stairs carrying a pair of pyjamas and a plate of cake. She knocked on the door of the spare bedroom Simon was staying in and went in. I crept along the landing and peeped inside.

Simon took the pyjamas from Mum and undid the top collar button on his shirt. Obviously he wasn't to know about her phobia.

Mum took several deep breaths. 'What's wrong?' Simon asked.

'Buttons,' Mum replied, panting heavily.

'Buttons? You're afraid of buttons?' Simon repeated.

'Do it up,' she shouted, pointing at his collar. 'Do it up!'

'Yes, of course,' he said, clumsily fiddling with the button. 'Sorry. There. Done.' Simon peered at Mum and, for the first time, noticed that her clothes were all fastened with zips – even her blouse. I laughed at Simon's expression of surprise.

'Who on earth is afraid of buttons?' Mum said softly, and she sat down on the bed. I felt a bit guilty for laughing then. I knew she hated her phobia. Mum had nearly choked on a button as a child and now she couldn't bear to touch them. Until I was four and could dress myself, all my clothes – including my underwear – were fastened with zips too.

Simon sat next to Mum on the bed, and I had to clap my hand over my mouth, because he hadn't sat down properly. He sort of perched, with only one part of his bum on the bed, and the rest just hovering in midair. He looked very uncomfortable.

'People are afraid of all sorts of things,' Simon said, and pretended not to notice how uncomfortable he was. 'Spiders, rats.' He coughed into his hand. 'Heights,' he added softly. 'Well, so I've heard. I mean, *I* don't know anyone—'

'Giraffes,' Mum interrupted.

Simon laughed at this. 'No, I don't think anyone's—'

'*I'm* afraid of giraffes,' she sighed. 'They've got suspiciously long necks.'

Simon didn't laugh at her like most people did. Instead, he smiled. And then Mum smiled back at him. A proper big grin that made her eyes sparkle. The tips of Simon's ears turned bright red again.

After a few moments of them just smiling at each other Mum pointed to the plate of cake. 'My signature dish,' she said. 'Leek surprise.'

Urgh. As well as 'going exotic' with them, Mum had a habit of putting vegetables in her cakes to make sure I was getting my five-a-day. Leek surprise was one of her worst.

Simon picked up the plate and made a show of tucking in. 'Ummm, it's . . . delicious,' he said eventually.

Mum looked unsure. Nobody ever liked her cakes. 'Really?' she asked.

'Yes,' Simon replied. 'Is that the surprise?'

Mum threw her head back and laughed loudly – even

louder than she laughed with Michael. I hadn't seen her laugh quite like that in a long time. Not since Dad died, anyway. Simon joined in, and the pair sat there laughing their heads off for what felt like ages. It wasn't even a good joke. My feet started to go numb; I was waiting so long for them to stop.

Mum took a tissue out of her pocket and dabbed tears from her eyes. She took a deep breath and regained her composure. 'Do you think we'll save Port Bren?' she asked softly.

'I'm sure you'll give it your best shot,' Simon replied. 'And that's all anyone can ask, isn't it?'

Well, that reply wasn't very clever, because it was exactly what Mum had said to me after I'd failed in the record attempt, so Simon was just copying. But Mum smiled at Simon and reached out and touched his hand. 'Thank you,' she said. She must have a short memory.

They sat there smiling for what felt like the longest time. Then I heard the heavy rattle of gold chains and saw Grandad Barry coming up the stairs, so I crept back to my room without having brushed my teeth, which made me feel all *urgh*, because Mum always said that if I ever forgot to brush them they'd all fall out when I was twenty-two.

Thursday
Chapter Seven

Three days left to save the village, and we hadn't had any other brilliant ideas. I had to think of new ways to put Port Bren on the map, so after I'd polished off my Weetabix Mum and I surfed the Internet for inspiration.

Mum replayed the video of the Spanish people throwing tomatoes at *La Tomatina* festival. Thousands of people ran through the streets of Spain, pelting tomatoes at one another, all laughing, all covered in slushy red pulp. It looked hilarious, though I knew it was never going to help us.

The phone in the kitchen rang, and we heard a *THUD* from upstairs. It was swiftly followed by a loud cry of 'RATS!' and Simon pounded down the stairs. He burst into the front room doing up his tie. Which was very smart of him, but he'd forgotten to put on his trousers, so he kind of ruined the professional look. 'Where's Barry?' Simon asked, panicked, not noticing his flowery orange boxer shorts on display. 'Is it for me?'

'Out jogging,' Mum replied, moving to answer the phone. 'And I'm not psychic.'

Simon checked his watch. 'Did Barry say when he'd be back?' he asked with a hint of urgency and desperation in his voice. Mostly desperation. 'My boss is very, uh, insistent.'

'You already said that,' Mum shouted from the kitchen. 'And, yes, it's for you.'

Who would be phoning Simon at our house? Curious, I wandered into the kitchen and pretended I was there to get a glass of milk.

Mum passed Simon the phone and left him to it. Simon took a deep breath. 'Hello?'

I could hear shouting from the other end. It was Max, his boss. 'I understand that, sir,' Simon said. 'If you just give me—' He pulled at his tie. 'Oh, an hour late already, is that so?'

I took the milk from the fridge and undid the cap.

Simon tried to undo his tie. 'If Devon could just hang on. The car's almost fixed.' Simon looked at me, then quickly turned his back and whispered into the phone. 'The mechanic said it will take another twenty minutes and then I'll be on my way.'

I was about to tell Simon that the mechanic was nowhere near fixing his car – in fact, the Marvel Barton mechanic didn't know anything about it – when water gushed out of the milk bottle. I'd forgotten I'd practised squirting milk from my eye earlier.

I mopped the kitchen counter with a cloth as Simon said, 'Thank you, sir. I won't let you down,' and put down the phone. He looked worried. 'Rats,' he muttered under his breath. He avoided my gaze, knowing I'd heard him tell a fib.

Simon went outside and sat on the garden wall. He hugged his briefcase to his chest, lost in thought. Just then, Gwyn walked past and stared at him. 'Morning!' Simon called, trying to muster a smile.

Gwyn opened her mouth in shock. 'Well, I never,' she said, and hurried off quickly, covering her eyes. 'You should be ashamed of yourself.'

Simon couldn't work out why she was so outraged. He spotted me at the front door. I laughed and pointed to his trousers. Or lack of them. He looked down and his face turned a bright shade of red as he saw his pale, twig-like legs on display. He leaped up in shock and his briefcase went flying. It came crashing down by the wall and its contents scattered everywhere. Simon barged past me as he raced into the house, leaving his case behind and tugging his shirt as low as he could.

At that moment a group of girls bounced past on space hoppers. I hid out of sight because one of the girls was Sarah Fielding, who always ate the paints during art and tried to play kiss chase with me. Sarah turned to the girl next to her. 'I can bounce further than you,' she yelled.

'Can't,' the girl shouted back. 'Look!' She launched off with a huge bounce and the space hopper went bounding down the road. It *was* pretty far, actually.

I watched them for a moment, and then my eyes fell on Simon's briefcase. The clipboard, stopwatch, tape measure and trundle wheel all lay strewn on the grass. Something in my mind whirred. *'One record break wouldn't be enough to put us on the map,'* I said slowly, remembering Simon's words from dinner the night before.

I looked again at Sarah as she space-hopped down the road, each bounce bigger than the one before. 'But what if we were *all* record breakers?' I cried. I picked up Simon's adjudicator tools where they'd landed by the garden wall and ran after Sarah and the girls as they bounced on. With the trundle wheel I measured the length of each bounce and noted it on Simon's clipboard.

I stalked behind the group while they bounced down the lane towards the village green, clicking my trundle wheel all the way. Just like a proper adjudicator.

After a few minutes Sarah looked behind her and caught me. 'Rats!' I hissed under my breath. She stopped bouncing and I quickly hid behind a wall.

'Luke Meldrum, is that you?' she called. She looked like she wanted to play kiss chase.

I held my breath for a few moments and tried not to make a sound. Then, when I thought the coast was clear, I stuck my head out from behind the wall and saw that the girls had gone. I grabbed the trundle wheel and scuttled off, sure I was on to A Good Thing.

As I walked along the lane and into the village high street, a massive Doberman darted past me. It wasn't as random as it sounds, because the dog belonged to an elderly man called Gareth, who didn't believe in leads for dogs. I took Simon's tape measure from my pocket and ran after the Doberman. It was far too fast, so I stopped by the village memorial statue, held the tape measure against it and measured that instead. I wrote down the height of the statue on the clipboard. I wasn't sure *exactly* what record attempts I was hoping the village could break, but I knew I had to at least try.

I came to a stop outside the village café, Pope Eggs Benedict, recently renamed after the owner's trip to the Vatican. Ordinarily I wasn't allowed in because Mum said that pie and mash was bad for your cholesterol and that I shouldn't encourage Grandad Barry, but I reasoned that this was for the village – it wasn't like I was going in for myself.

The café was packed, so I squeezed into a chair at Trevor's table, and pondered what records could be broken there. Fastest time to fry an egg? Greasiest sausage? As I thought about it, I watched Trevor eat. Trevor, who had a belly bigger than Grandad Barry's, was shoving doughnuts into his mouth as fast as he could, which was how Trevor always ate. He said that after growing up with seven brothers and four sisters, if he didn't eat fast at dinner time, he didn't eat at all. Sugar and jam and large quantities of spittle flew from Trevor's mouth as he wolfed down the doughnuts, and I picked up a newspaper from the table to shield myself from the shower.

Surely there was something in Trevor's quick eating? Most in a minute, perhaps? The current world record for a minute's quick-doughnut-eating was seven. I grabbed Simon's stopwatch from my pocket and clicked it and watched Trevor intensely as he bit into doughnut after doughnut, with no telling when – or if – he was going to stop. Four, now five doughnuts . . . Jam oozed out of them, dribbling down Trevor's shirt, but he ploughed on regardless. Six. Trevor looked up and caught me staring at him. I buried myself further inside the newspaper. Seven doughnuts! He was almost there.

I looked down at the stopwatch – sixty seconds had passed, so I clicked it under the table. I peered out from the side of the newspaper and counted the remains of dough-nuts on Trevor's plate. Eight doughnuts! Trevor had done it! The most doughnuts eaten in one minute, and Trevor hadn't even broken into a sweat. Or stopped. Trevor continued to cram the doughnuts into his mouth, picking the spilled jam off his T-shirt.

I punched the air in excitement. 'Yessssssssss!' This could *really* work!

I ran out of the café, all the way home and burst through the door. From the hall I could hear Mum singing in the shower. I shouted through the house. 'Simon?'

Simon popped his head round the kitchen door and motioned that he was on the phone. He looked nervous – more so than normal. He held the phone away from his ear again and I could hear shouting from the other end. Again. I held Simon's clipboard up to him, and attempted to show him Trevor's efforts. Simon was too busy apologizing to his boss to notice. 'Yes, sir,' he stuttered into the phone. 'The mechanic *was* meant to be finished by now . . .'

I stepped forward. 'Simon?' I said. 'I know how we can save the village.'

Simon waved me away with a flick of his hand. *How rude!*

'I know this was my last chance, sir,' he whispered, 'but I should be on the road in half an hour.'

Another fib. Still, I knew that persistency was the name of the game. 'Trevor's eaten doughnuts,' I repeated. Simon motioned for me to be quiet and turned his back on me. Well, really.

'I can explain, sir,' Simon stammered. He was getting more and more flustered by the second. 'Please don't sack me.'

I rolled my eyes. And then I spotted my world records DVD with Vinnie Denton's grinning face on the sideboard. I picked up the DVD and waved it at Simon. 'More records,' I said.

Simon pulled at his tie again and gulped. 'Why am I late?' he repeated into the phone. I could see the panic in his eyes. 'It's, uh, because, uh . . .' Simon scanned the room, desperately searching for inspiration.

I waved the DVD again. 'More records,' I repeated.

Simon looked at me in confusion. Slowly, it clicked into place. 'More records?' he asked, surprised.

I nodded. *Finally!* For a professional man, he was a little slow on the uptake.

'More records?' boomed Max's voice down the line.

I showed the clipboard to Simon once more and he looked at it curiously. 'Uh, yes, sir,' he said into the phone. 'They're doing more records. No, not just the boy.' He coughed. 'Uh, how many?' Simon looked at me and I spread my hands wide open. 'Uh, all of them?' Simon said into the phone. He wiped his forehead with his sleeve. 'Yes, all of them. The whole village!'

Simon waited for a response from his boss. I stood with bated breath. This *had* to work.

Eventually Simon gave me a wink. 'Yesssssssss!' I said, and punched the air with my fist. I'd been doing a lot of that lately.

'Yes, sir,' Simon said, breathing a sigh of relief. 'I'll keep you posted.' He hung up the phone, took his hanky from his pocket and patted his face with it. 'That was a close shave.' He smiled at me. 'What gave you this idea?'

I shrugged. 'You said one record break wouldn't be enough. And then I remembered Ashrita Furman. If he's famous for being the person with the most world records, surely being the village with the most records broken would be something, wouldn't it?'

Simon nodded. 'It would be a world first. And I believe it would be enough to put you on the map, yes.'

'And save the village and our homes and the grave-yard?'

'All those things, yes,' Simon replied with a big grin. 'Do you think the rest of the village will be up for it?'

I thought for a moment. They might, considering none of their other protests had worked. But I also knew that I'd failed in my record attempt and if I, king of all things records, couldn't do it, I'd have a hard job convincing the rest of the village. Not to mention Mum.

Then I remembered what Dad had always told me about trying to break world records. Only the very best could do it. It required training, dedication, commitment. Not everyone was record-breaking material. 'Trevor's really good at eating,' I said, 'which is why he could cram all the doughnuts into his mouth, but what records can other people try for?'

Simon gestured to one of my record books on the sideboard. 'You can break records for all sorts of things,' he replied. 'Half the time, people don't even realize how talented and unique and special they really are.'

I frowned. That wasn't what Dad had said.

The sound of Mum's singing drifted down from the bathroom. Simon beckoned to me and we walked upstairs. 'Take your mum, for instance,' he said. He stopped on the landing outside the bathroom, and took out a decibel-reader from his pocket. From inside, Mum sang her heart out as she took a shower. She loved singing, and always sang as loud as she could. The trouble was, she was about as good at singing as she was at baking cakes.

I grimaced as what sounded like a bag of cats being squashed came from behind the bathroom door. 'She's not the best singer,' I muttered.

Simon pointed to the decibel-reader in his hand. The little red arrow on the reader moved between several numbers, indicating how loud the singing was. 'No,' he agreed, 'but she could be the loudest.' He jotted something down on his clipboard: *Loudest note*.

Mum hit a particularly high note and Simon jumped in shock and dropped his clipboard. As he bent to pick it up, the door opened and Mum stood there in a towel, her pale skin glistening with water. 'What's all this?' she demanded.

Simon blushed and held his clipboard out to her. 'Most doughnuts in a minute,' he stuttered.

'Doughnuts?'

'And Trevor didn't even know he was attempting it.'

Mum raised her eyebrows at Simon. 'Why are you doing this?' she asked.

Simon cleared his throat. 'For the village. To put you on the map and contest the waste plant.' He gave me a wink. No need to mention the saving-his-job part, either.

'Trevor's already broken one,' I piped up. I thought for a second, and then quickly added, 'And it wasn't dangerous!'

Grandad Barry plodded up the stairs. 'You think this will work, do you?' he asked, having overheard everything. Maybe I got my Bat Ears from him, after all.

'I don't see why it wouldn't be historic,' Simon replied. 'I could stay.' He tugged at his tie nervously. 'To, uh, to adjudicate.'

I couldn't believe what an excellent plan we'd formulated. We were doing more records. We were going to save the village. And a real live record adjudicator was going to stay and help.

'Brilliant!' I said, the happiest I'd been for a long time. Or at least since I'd failed my last record attempt. And then, before I knew what I was doing, I reached out and gave Simon a hug. I threw my arms around him and gave him a really good squeeze. 'It's just so exciting!' I cried.

Simon looked really surprised, but sort of patted my head in return.

I saw Mum narrow her eyes at me, so I untangled myself. 'I'll get my books!' I yelled.

I started to run off to my bedroom, but Mum blocked my path. 'No,' she said firmly, and pulled her towel tighter around her. 'You tried once, now that's it. Leave it to the rest of the village.'

I opened my mouth in surprise. 'But it's my idea!'

'No buts!' Mum replied. 'You can read the books and watch the DVDs, but no more record attempts for you, young man.'

I couldn't believe it. It was, quite possibly, the most brilliant idea in the history of Port Bren, and it was mine! All mine! And yet here was Mum telling me I couldn't even act on it.

'But, Mum,' I protested, trying hard not to glare at her.

'But nothing,' Mum replied, before I could even finish. 'Conversation's over. It's down to Simon.' She padded down the landing back to her room.

I frowned. It was pointless trying to argue with Mum any more, but this wasn't the last of it. The village's fate in Simon's hands? Not if I had anything to do with it.

Chapter Eight

Wearing a different special-occasion toupee (Christmas), Grandad Barry raced around the village, spreading the news of the multiple record attempts. 'We're Team GB,' he insisted on saying, having watched one too many Olympic commentaries in his life. 'Eat your heart out, Seb Coe!'

The villagers – and Mr Pringle-Bliss – seemed happy to go along with the plan, no questions asked. Except for Glyn, who kept asking what Seb's toe had to do with anything.

With the village on board, Simon sat on the sofa in our front room with his clipboard in hand, holding court. A single file of villagers stood in front of him. I hovered at the door, listening as everyone chattered excitedly about the new plan to save the village. *My* plan.

Glyn leaned on his walking stick at the front of the queue and looked as if he was about to burst into tears. 'But I've always wanted to,' he sniffed, his bottom lip trembling.

'I'm sorry,' Simon replied, 'but technically, I *don't* think you should eat lead.'

Even though I knew that, for nearly half a century, Michel Lotito of Grenoble, France, had eaten a kilogram of metal and glass every day, I realized it was probably quite sensible for Glyn not to attempt it. He could barely handle his medication.

Daffydd moved to the front of the queue. Daffydd had a white beard, always looked rather jolly and spoke with a lilting Welsh accent. Largely to do with the fact that he *was* Welsh. He had a voice that boomed as loud as a cannon, which is why he always played Father Christmas at the Winter Fair, even though Grandad Barry wanted the part. He never said so in public, but I knew Grandad Barry was furious that a mainlander had landed the Santa gig.

Daffydd pointed to a group of twenty men behind him, all wearing matching bright blue cardigans. 'Our male choir once did a contest for *Songs of Praise*,' he said. 'We came second.'

Simon was impressed. 'Really?' he asked. 'Out of how many choirs?'

'Just us,' Daffydd replied. 'We were robbed.'

Grandad Barry jostled his way to the front of the line and dug his elbow into Daffydd's ribs. 'Out of the way, Daffydd,' he commanded.

Daffydd rubbed his side in outrage. 'You do know what

letter comes between P and R in the alphabet, do you, Barry?'

Grandad Barry turned to him, confused. 'Q,' he replied.

'Yes,' Daffydd seethed, pointing to the line of villagers behind him. 'There is. Use it.'

Grandad Barry rolled his eyes and ignored him, instead motioning to Simon's clipboard. 'I'm the Mayor,' he boomed, a broad grin on his face.

Simon waited for something else to be said. The clock on the mantelpiece ticked loudly as a full minute passed. 'Uh, just being the Mayor isn't strictly an attempt, Barry,' Simon said eventually. 'Sorry.'

Grandad Barry's smile faltered a little. 'Are you sure? I've been elected Mayor of Port Bren nineteen years in a—'

'Yes!' Simon interrupted. 'I know. It's not an attempt.'

Grandad Barry clutched at his ceremonial chains in shock. 'But what else can I do?' he asked.

No one said anything for a while and I realized that this was my chance. The village *needed* me. I ran into the room and grabbed my record book from 2011. 'Here,' I said, and pointed to a page. 'Fastest time to drink a pint of ale. You could do that.'

'Oh, no,' Grandad Barry said mournfully. 'Your mum's put me on a diet. No alcohol, no chocolate, no carbs after two. I'm living on lentils and wheatgrass.' He leaned in to whisper to Simon, but I could hear everything. 'And prawn crackers,' he added, 'but she doesn't know about them.'

Well, that's a bit rich, I thought, seeing as I wasn't meant to be encouraging him.

Mum emerged from the back of the crowd, holding a cake stand with another of her exotic creations on it. Michael had his arm round her, and he took a sip from his cup of tea.

I looked at it closely. 'That's Dad's mug,' I said to him.

Michael looked down at it in surprise. 'Oh yes, *World's Best Dad*,' he said. 'So it is.' I waited for him to apologize, but he didn't.

'Can you get another mug, please?' I asked him eventually.

Michael opened his mouth to say something but Mum leaped in. 'What are you doing here, Luke?' she asked me. 'You're not to get involved in this.'

I started to protest, but Mum gave me one of her *Watch it, sunshine* looks. Michael just shrugged his shoulders and sipped from Dad's mug again.

I slunk out the room, sat down halfway up the stairs and put my head in my hands. Not only had my world-records fun been spoiled once more, but Michael had used Dad's mug. And Mum had let him. She knew no one was meant to touch Dad's mug but me. He wasn't *her* World's Best Dad, was he?

'Put me down for a spot of boxing,' I heard Grandad Barry say back in the front room. 'That'll do.'

I watched through the glass-panelled wall as Simon added Grandad Barry's attempt to the list and totted them all up. 'Well, that makes seventy-four proposed attempts,' he said.

'And we've got to break fifty world records to save the village?' Grandad Barry asked.

Mr Pringle-Bliss stepped out from the crowd of villagers. 'That's what the council considers "historic", so I'm told,' he said, and blew into his handkerchief. 'Being the village with the most records broken would be historic enough to stop the waste plant being built.'

The villagers started congratulating each other on such a marvellous plan to save their homes, but nobody bothered to thank me for it.

'But there has to be a time limit,' Mr Pringle-Bliss interrupted and everyone stopped what they were doing. 'The council are giving you till eight a.m. Sunday. You've got to break fifty world records by then.'

Grandad Barry raised his arm to Simon. 'Well, what are we waiting for? Over to you, Simon David.'

79

'Right,' Simon said, leaping up from the sofa. 'Does anyone have any questions?'

A sea of hands shot up.

'Will we do it?'

'Will we break fifty records by Sunday?'

'Why have you got two first names?'

That last one was me. I was still desperate to know and had shouted it from the stairs, but Simon hadn't heard.

Simon looked over to Mum, who munched on a slice of her banana and turnip cake and worked intently on another SAVE PORT BREN placard. 'Any more for any more?' Simon asked, but Mum pretended not to hear. 'Right,' Simon nodded. 'I'll phone HQ. Get everything confirmed.'

As Simon left the room, Grandad Barry turned to the rest of the villagers. 'Now, let's get training,' he said, with a spring in his step. He motioned for everyone to follow him and led them all out into the front garden. 'We need to be as strong, as fit and as supple as we can. We'll leave no stone unturned.' Grandad Barry pointed to a small rock. 'Except for that one, it's got a family of snails underneath it.' He clapped his hands. 'Let's do it!' he boomed.

I leaned out of my bedroom window and watched glumly as the villagers embarked on their training regime, running down to the children's playground at the back of the village green. Jimmy performed fifty chin-ups on the monkey bars in one minute, though no one noticed that Gwyn was standing underneath him and pushing Jimmy's knees to help. Grandad Barry managed six press-ups and The Other Barry did fourteen squat-thrusts before collapsing.

Cheryl, the baker, and Roy Fort, the butcher, and his son stood to one side tooting their musical instruments. Something that sounded like 'Jingle Bells' squawked out. 'Why don't you play something to rally the crowd, hey?' Grandad Barry called out to them. 'Give us "Eye of the Tiger"!'

Roy's son thought for a moment and signalled to the rest of the band. Then they launched heartily into a new song. It still sounded like 'Jingle Bells'.

The dad of one of the boys in my class strapped himself into a harness and attached it to a wooden crate. He ordered three small lads to sit on top of the crate and then started pulling with all of his might, staggering forward across the green. His eyes bulged with the effort, and even from my window I saw a vein throbbing in his neck. The dad cried out in anguish. 'Adrian!' he yelled, clearly in pain. 'Adriaaaaaaaaaaaaaaan!'

Adrian ran forward with a towel and patted it round his dad's face. 'Thanks, son,' he said, straining.

Then Glyn moved to join in with everyone, but his

walking stick accidentally got stuck in the wheel of the roundabout. He struggled round and round, unable to get off. I couldn't help myself, and laughed out loud at the funny sight of the villagers, despite feeling sad.

Next stop was the village hall, and I leaned as far as I could out of the window without risking death to watch Glyn, Gwyn and Jimmy stagger up the steps. They each carried a pole, with a big plastic bottle of water attached to either end, on their shoulders. Grandad Barry looked on from the top step.

'How does this help?' Glyn asked as he reached the top and dropped his pole at Grandad Barry's feet, clearly exhausted.

Grandad Barry detached a water bottle and glugged greedily. 'It doesn't,' he replied, smacking his lips. 'I was just thirsty.'

Jimmy had to restrain Glyn as he lunged at Grandad Barry. 'Blow this for a game of tiddlywinks,' Glyn huffed, and stumbled back down the steps. 'I've got something else up my sleeve.'

I couldn't bear to watch any more. I hated being so tantalizingly close to the world-record attempts but forbidden from taking part. I needed to get out.

I ran down the stairs, through the front door and picked up my bike from the garden. From inside the front room,

Mum tapped on the window. 'I'm warning you,' she called.

I let out all my breath in one big huff. I knew I wasn't allowed to get involved, so I wished she'd just stop banging on about it.

I pedalled down the lane next to Dead Glyn's farmland. All I wanted was to clear my head and forget about records. *What was the point if I couldn't do anything?*

But forgetting about records was never going to be possible, because Port Bren had gone record-breaking mad.

As I turned the corner, I saw everyone from the village racing towards me, stampeding like cattle. They all had barmy grins plastered on their faces and pushed each other out of the way as they scrambled to their next training session. Elbows were poked in ribs. Feet were trodden on. One villager crowd-surfed his way past. It was chaos.

I darted to one side to avoid being squashed, and watched as everyone ran to the small village shop. It had been owned by Grandad Barry since 1972 – though that wasn't a world record – and sold everything a villager would ever need. Even stuff a villager wouldn't – Grandad Barry was particularly proud of a batch of glass eyes he'd recently had imported from Stockholm.

Curiosity – all right, nosiness – got the better of me, and I pedalled off to find out what they were doing.

'You OK, Luke?' Martin's mum nodded to me as she

83

darted into Grandad Barry's shop. 'This is right up your street, isn't it?'

I didn't say anything. All the mums of the boys in my class dashed into the shop and stashed tins of baked beans in their shopping baskets. And that just made me really sad, because everyone else's mum was happy for them to join in. Everyone's except mine.

As the mums were gathering their tins, Gareth, one of Grandad Barry's friends from the lawn bowls club and owner of the free-roaming Doberman, wandered into the shop.

This in itself caused everyone to stop what they were doing. Even though they were friends, Grandad Barry had banned Gareth from entering, thanks to Gareth's exploits seven years ago when he'd worn a balaclava and tried to hold up Jane, the cashier, at gunpoint. Except he'd forgotten the gun. And he'd worn his bowling-club shirt with *Gareth 'Spinner' Stephens* on the back, so he'd kind of given the game away.

Gareth picked up a shopping basket and marched over to the mums at the baked-bean shelf. But he was too late – there was only one tin left!

All the villagers in the shop held their breath as Gareth and one mum prepared to battle it out for the last tin of baked beans. No one was going to budge. It was like one of those showdowns in Westerns where two cowboys stare at each other, waiting to see who will be the first to fire. Except here no one had a gun (again).

Just when they couldn't take it any more, the mum leaped forward, threw herself onto the baked-bean shelf and clutched at the tin. Gareth pounced on top of her and tried to tickle her until she let go, but she was pretty strong. Then again, she was Sarah Fielding's mother, so I expected nothing less – Grandad Barry said it ran in the family.

Eventually Gareth realized he wasn't going to win. 'Fine,' he scowled and got to his feet. 'I'll find something else to bathe in.' He gave an indignant huff and stormed out of the shop.

Grandad Barry walked past carrying an enormous pile of paper. 'What's that for?' I asked.

'The paper-shredding attempt,' he replied. 'It's finally given me an excuse to get rid of all the damn bills I get sent.'

'I've got some old posters you can have,' I suggested. 'From my room.'

'Thanks, son, but your mum won't want you to help. Sorry.' I looked down at my trainers. 'You know what she's like when she gets an idea in her head,' Grandad Barry continued. 'But it's only because she loves you so much.' He ruffled my hair and jogged away.

The villagers streamed out of the shop, racing back to their homes to gather as many newspapers, bank statements and those annoying junk-mail leaflets that claim you've won a million pounds as they could carry.

Michael wasn't participating in this event, but stood on the edge of his father's land, lost in thought. I pedalled over to him. 'Are you not getting involved in this, either?' I asked.

He looked distracted. 'What?'

'Have you got any paper to shred? They need as much as they can, short of knocking down a forest,' I replied. 'The world's current record for the most paper shredded in one hour is three tonnes, seventy-two kilograms.'

Michael gazed into the distance. He looked like he had a lot on his mind. 'Michael?' I asked again.

Michael stared down at me in surprise, as if he'd only then noticed my presence. 'Sure,' he said after a moment. 'Take any leaflets and newspapers you can find.'

'I didn't mean me—' I started to say, but then I stopped. I thought over Michael's unintentional suggestion – perhaps I could get the papers from his house and help that way, and Mum wouldn't need to know. 'Uh, thanks,' I said quickly, and left before he could catch on.

I rang the doorbell of Michael's mansion. Overlooking the harbour, it was luckily one of the few houses in the village that wouldn't be demolished by the waste plant. Though Grandad Barry thought that wouldn't be such a bad idea. 'Too ostentatious,' he once said to me of Michael's house, but that was before Michael had started dating Mum and before I'd had the dictionary to look up what the word meant.

Michael's housekeeper, Doris, opened the door. 'Another one of Mr Harding's schemes, I suppose?' she said, frowning. She was really stern looking and always pursed her lips together when she spoke. But Michael seemed to like her. She'd been with him ever since he'd moved back to the island and built his mansion six years ago. 'Perks of Jersey being a tax haven,' Grandad Barry had said.

I set about finding all the papers that looked like junk. I checked the front room, then the first floor, including the kitchen, and then made my way up to Michael's study on the fourth floor. I couldn't stop smiling as I worked. I was finally getting involved in the attempts.

Michael's study was a large room lined with oak bookshelves and with a mahogany desk in the corner. I rummaged through a bundle of papers on the desktop. They all looked quite official, so I knew not to shred those. Then my eye fell upon a particularly fancy piece of paperwork. I knew I probably shouldn't read Michael's private stuff, but curiosity got the better of me – all right, nosiness.

I checked that no one could see and then held the paper up to the light. It had an elaborate and official-looking stamp in the left-hand corner made up of three curling green leaves. There was a bulk of text in the middle of the page and as my eyes skimmed down, I saw *DEEDS TO THE LAND* written in bold. Underneath was Michael's signature.

As I tried to work out what that meant, I heard a creak on the landing outside the study. I quickly stuffed the paperwork back in amongst the pile and made my way towards the door.

Michael burst into the study. He'd clearly been running. 'There's nothing in here,' he panted in between breaths.

I nodded. 'Yeah, I know. I've already got these.' I held up a bunch of takeaway menus I'd found in the kitchen. All of them were for the only takeaway restaurant this side of Marvel Barton, which had to specialize in Chinese, Indian and Italian food just to keep everyone happy. It was the first Chinese-Indian-Italian restaurant in Jersey. With chips.

'Actually, Luke,' Michael said, 'while you're here. I thought we could all have dinner at mine tonight; you, me, your mum, Grandad Barry. What do you reckon?'

I checked my watch. 'They'll probably be mid-attempts by then.'

'I understand that, but you need to eat,' Michael replied,

his heavy black eyebrows knitted into a frown. 'I'm sure you can spare an hour to get to know your mum's boyfriend.' He thought for a moment and then winked at me. 'Though perhaps I won't be her boyfriend for much longer.'

I opened my mouth in surprise. 'Is Mum going to dump you?'

'That's not what I meant,' Michael laughed.

I checked my watch again. 'They'll be starting the attempts soon. Can Simon come?'

'I don't think so.'

Well, that wasn't much help. 'I'm not allowed to get involved in the records, so I haven't really spent much time with him,' I said.

'You can spend time with me,' Michael replied, looking put out.

I shrugged. 'It's not the same. You don't know about records.'

Michael wasn't particularly impressed by this. He'd tried to extend a friendly gesture to me and here I was, banging on about Simon all the time. I knew that Simon wasn't exactly Michael's idea of a fun party guest – or any sort of party guest – but I didn't care. I could innocently ask Simon about records over dinner and Mum wouldn't be able to say anything.

Michael sighed. 'Fine,' he said after a moment. 'I'll see you all later.'

I left Michael's study with a strange feeling. My earlier jubilation at finally getting involved in the record attempts had given way to something else. I couldn't quite put my finger on it, but something was bugging me. Something to do with the paperwork I'd seen.

Chapter Nine

I pedalled back to our house, deep in thought. I was clever; I knew that, especially when it came to maths and numbers, but I didn't know what the deeds meant.

The villagers were still getting ready for their record attempts. A little way up the lane, Grandad Barry attempted a sit-up. Jimmy held his ankles and waggled a bar of chocolate to entice him to go faster. Except there wasn't much chocolate left because Jimmy kept eating it every time Grandad Barry wasn't looking.

A little further along, Walking Stick Glyn was in the middle of a heated argument with Adam Leroux, the farmer who owned all the cows in Port Bren. All four of them.

'I don't care,' Adam stated firmly, his arms crossed in front of him. 'You're not recreating the Pamplona Running of the Bulls with my Jersey cows.'

Glyn shook his head in despair and then spotted me. 'It's all your mum's fault,' he sighed, wagging a finger at me accusingly. 'After she showed us that *La Tomatina* video I looked on the Internet for other things we could do and thought that running in front of a raging bull trying not to get gorged would be just the ticket.'

I frowned. 'But we don't have any bulls,' I replied, and then pointed to his walking stick. 'And you can't run.'

Glyn threw up his arms in frustration. 'Which is why I wanted the cows!' he yelled, and he shuffled off as fast as his walking stick would take him. Which wasn't very.

'Running in front of a cow isn't even a world record!' I called after him, but he didn't hear me.

I sighed heavily. It was clear that the villagers didn't have a clue what they were doing. I knew I *had* to get involved in the record attempts, somehow. The village needed me. I knew more about records than anyone. Except Simon, but Simon wasn't allowed to get involved because he was an adjudicator. I couldn't leave the village's fate in his hands.

It came to me in a flash. I *would* get involved, but I'd have to do it in secret. I'd help the village, but I'd have to sneak around and not let Mum know. I felt terrible knowing that I'd be going behind her back, but it was for a good cause. The *best* cause.

I raced back home and burst into my bedroom. I opened the wardrobe and started flinging clothes about. If I was going to get involved in secret, I needed a disguise. Think James Bond. Batman. The Flaming Carrot.

Less than an hour later everyone made their way to the church, which was to be the launch pad for all the record attempts.

Wearing one of Grandad Barry's sheepskin coats, which swamped me in its enormity, and glasses from a detective kit Mum had bought me a few years ago, I snuck into the back of the church, where villagers packed the pews, chatting loudly to one another. All right, so I was hardly James Bond, but I didn't have much to work with. I'd also managed to sneak one of Grandad Barry's special-occasion toupees (Halloween) from his bedroom, though it felt all hot and itchy on my head. I slid into a pew next to Glyn, who was frantically sketching a map of Adam's farmland on a notepad and drawing all sorts of arrows and diagrams on it. I caught the words 'pneumatic drill'.

I leaned over and whispered to him, 'Glyn, what does the word deeds mean?'

Glyn looked at me and jumped in surprise. He squinted in my face and I lifted my glasses. 'Luke?' he asked, confused.

I nodded. 'I'm in disguise.'

Glyn tapped his nose softly with his index finger. 'Mum's the word,' he whispered.

'*Deeds?*' I repeated. 'What does that word mean?'

93

But before Glyn could answer, Grandad Barry bounded to the front of the congregation and motioned for silence. 'Thank you, thank you, everyone for coming,' he boomed in his most solemn voice. It was the voice he used for momentous occasions such as these. The last time he'd used it had been back in 'ninety-four – the year of that unpleasant business when he'd failed to be re-elected as Port Bren Mayor. No one was allowed to mention the unpleasant business of 'ninety-four in our house, but it had something to do with a clerical error which meant that Basil Worsley had been elected Mayor instead of Grandad Barry. Much to everyone's surprise, as Basil Worsley had died two years *before* the election.

'We all know how important this is to us,' Grandad Barry continued. 'To our history. Our community. To those we've loved and lost along the way. And now, like a salad, or indeed a caber in a highland-games contest, the gauntlet has been tossed. So let us all—'

'Barry,' The Other Barry interrupted as he realized Grandad Barry didn't half go on. 'We've only got three days.'

'Right you are.' Grandad Barry frowned. 'Sixty-five hours to save Port Bren. Let the attempts begin!'

Daffydd and his male choir took their positions at the front of the church, all wearing matching red cardigans ready for their longest continual chorus record attempt.

Simon gave them the nod and clicked his stopwatch, and the choir launched heartily into 'Land of Our Fathers', Daffydd's favourite hymn.

It was Welsh. Grandad Barry almost spat in disgust, but realized he couldn't in a house of God. 'Mainlanders,' he muttered under his breath.

The villagers streamed out of the church towards the village green and we passed Mum on the way. Adamant that she wanted nothing to do with our record attempts she'd plonked herself down on Dead Glyn's farmland and, as the strains of the choir rang out, hammered her SAVE PORT BREN placard into the ground.

'Come on, love,' Grandad Barry soothed. 'Why not join in, eh?'

Mum shook her head. 'This is my protest,' she stated firmly, and motioned to her placard. 'And I'm going to try and persuade the council on my own. Without trying to break records.'

'How?' Grandad Barry asked.

Mum avoided his gaze. 'I'm going to bake them a cake,' she said eventually. Nobody said anything for a moment.

Then the whole village erupted with laughter. 'Bake them a cake!' Walking-Stick Glyn howled as tears ran down his cheeks. 'You!'

'We want them to help us, love,' Grandad Barry laughed. 'Not put them off altogether.'

Mum shrugged it off. 'You'll see,' she said in a stern voice. 'I'll get Luke to help me.'

I panicked. 'Poor lad,' Glyn whispered to me. 'Good luck.'

I ducked my head down and merged myself into the rest of the crowd as they made their way onwards.

Walking down to the harbour, the atmosphere amongst the villagers was electric. Everyone had massive grins on their faces. Never in the history of Port Bren had such an important and exciting series of events taken place.

In amongst the fishing boats and dinghies, a few of the sportier residents of Port Bren were windsurfing and swimming, ready for their water-based record attempts.

Mr Wilson, the headmistress's husband, sat in a canoe with a rucksack on his back. Mrs Wilson stood on the shoreline and wiped a tear from her eye. 'Have you got your reading glasses?' she called to him. He gave her a thumbs-up.

'Away you go!' Simon shouted, waving him off.

Mr Wilson grinned, picked up his oar and started paddling out to sea. 'I'll see you in a few days!' he yelled. 'Don't worry, I've got life insurance!'

'Just keep the ticker-counter going so we can measure

the distance,' Simon shouted back, and he marked on his clipboard: *Furthest distance in a canoe.*

That's when we heard the splash.

The crowd gasped as we saw the canoe upturned in the distance, Mr Wilson frantically doggy-paddling alongside. 'I'm OK!' he yelled. 'Don't worry about me!'

'How can you fall out of a canoe?' someone at the back of the crowd whispered.

Simon looked around the villagers. 'You're all going to have to do better than this if you've any chance of breaking fifty records,' he said firmly.

The crowd quietened down and, as Mr Wilson took off for a second time, we left the harbour in a distinctly more sombre mood than when we'd arrived mere moments ago.

As ever, the village green was the hub of the action, and the villagers had taken over every inch of it. Simon was now standing in the middle of the green waiting for us to set up the attempts. In his glass case, Sir Walter watched from the sidelines.

Last to arrive on the green, Dave, who was incredibly old – absurdly old, in fact – clutched a piece of paper and walked slowly towards Simon. He seemed desperate to reach him, but took for ever because his old age slowed him down.

Jimmy sat on a stool to one side of the green and held his

arms in the air, ready for his 'Most T-shirts worn' attempt.

His mum placed a T-shirt over his head and pulled it down. She put another one over his head. Then another. And another. She had a whole mound of T-shirts ready to go.

I snuck onto the green and hid out of sight, behind the yellow medieval-fortress bouncy castle. On it, eighteen pensioners bounced, aided by their walking sticks. They were so enthusiastic, it was easy to forget most of them had arthritis.

Having lost his fight for the last tin of baked beans in Grandad Barry's shop, Gareth had indeed found something else to bathe in. From a cardboard box with air holes punched into it, he took out seven black snakes and placed them in an empty tin bathtub, which he'd positioned in the middle of the green. With one dramatic flick he whipped off his trousers, revealing his swimming trunks. A tight, unattractive, frayed pair of lime-green swimming trunks. Gareth slowly lowered himself into the bath. Admittedly this was all a little odd, but Port Bren was full of strange people, so nobody batted an eye.

Elsewhere on the green, forty-seven dogs of assorted breeds were tied to a wooden post and a group of Brownies started lathering them with buckets of soap and water. Five dart players practised their aim in front of makeshift dart boards. Next to them seven men balanced on unicycles, tossing pancakes in pans.

In front of a wooden board with measurements running up it Victoria, the stocky girl from my class, twirled a baton in her hand. Every so often she would toss the baton up into the air and then attempt to catch it. The height part was great – the way she was going, Victoria was well on target to breaking the 'Highest baton tossed' record. The only trouble was, she wasn't very good at the catching part and innocent passers-by kept being struck on the head by a wayward baton.

Jimmy struggled under the weight of wearing sixty-one T-shirts. 'Are we nearly there yet?' he asked his mum as he fidgeted on his stool. 'I need to wee.'

She sighed. 'Just stay still. It's only for the time being.' She accidentally knocked his glasses off his head as she pulled another T-shirt on him.

Jimmy frowned. 'I *hate* the time being,' he replied.

In the middle of the green, Simon peered into Gareth's bathtub. The snakes lay motionless. Simon took his pen from the inside pocket of his jacket and prodded a snake, ever so gently. It didn't move. 'Uh, sitting in a bath with *plastic* snakes isn't strictly an attempt,' he informed Gareth.

Gareth shrugged. 'Didn't want to use real ones, did I?' he replied, wincing. 'Can't stand creepy-crawlies.'

Simon shook his head in disbelief and moved on. A definite fail!

I poked my head out from behind the bouncy castle and watched the villagers in their attempts. I knew I had to do something. Everyone was trying, but they were all a bit hopeless. I had my disguise – I just had to find the opportunity.

Simon approached the dart players' board and looked down at the makeshift throwing line they'd taped to the floor. 'The oche seems a bit close to the dart board,' he said, and reached into his pocket for his tape measure.

'That's the point,' one of the players replied. 'We want to break the record, you know.'

Simon sighed. 'I know, but officially the throwing distance should be two point three metres.' The dart players all blustered round him, looking like they were ready for a fight.

Just then, Gwyn called out to Simon. 'Ready!' she trilled as, smack bang in the middle of the green, she hula-hooped energetically, 104 hoops around her waist. Anyone else would have been weighed down under so many, but Gwyn looked like she was having the time of her life. 'My hips haven't seen this sort of action in thirty years!' she cried breathlessly.

'That's what she says,' a villager muttered to her

neighbour. Simon left his tape measure at the oche, and he and the dart players moved towards Gwyn.

Suddenly Mum marched onto the green, waving her SAVE PORT BREN placard around. A few villagers rolled their eyes at her continued protest, but Mum ignored them. I ducked out of sight. Part of me resented her being there, spoiling my fun, even though I knew Mum was only trying to help in her own way. I watched as Simon chatted to Gwyn and offered her words of encouragement. That, I thought, was what *I* should be doing.

Simon gave Gwyn the nod – it was time for her 'Most hula hoops in one minute' attempt. Hula-hooping with all of her might, Gwyn swung her hips, and hula hoops from the top of her tummy to the top of her knees swung round and round, so fast they became a blur.

That was when I seized the opportunity.

With the dart players and all the villagers surrounding Gwyn, I raced over to the dart board and, glancing round to check no one was watching, picked up the line of tape from the ground. I grabbed the tape measure and quickly paced the required 2.3 metres. I stuck the tape down again and stepped back to admire my handiwork.

Just then, Simon glanced over to the dart board and peered at the newly formed oche. I froze as he locked eyes with me and I could see him study my face. But after a moment he simply turned his attention back to Gwyn.

In what felt like no time at all, Simon clicked his stop-watch – sixty seconds had passed. Simon raised his head and stared at the villagers. They all stared back at him in hope, holding their breath as one.

Simon's face broke into a grin. Gwyn had completed the attempt and broken the record! I shouted my delight. 'Yessssssssss!' I leaped in the air. Mum glanced behind her, but I ducked back behind the bouncy castle just in time.

'After Trevor's doughnut-eating record, which I verified personally this morning,' Simon stated to the crowd, 'Port Bren has now successfully broken its second world record.'

The crowd cheered once more. 'Are we keeping a tally?' Gwyn asked. 'So we know how we're getting on?'

Simon gestured to his clipboard. 'It's on here.'

'I meant something we could all see?'

Simon shrugged. 'I'll leave that up to you.'

He tapped his watch and motioned to the Year Five and Six boys from my school, all preparing for the loudest burp attempt. Full from beans and Brussels sprouts and fizzy pop, they all stood in a line, clutching their stomachs. All except me.

As sad as I was that I'd been forbidden from taking part, I was much more sad at the fact that this was something else that would make me different from my friends. Everyone had been a little strange with me since Dad had died. Like Jimmy. They didn't talk to me much. Nobody came over to play any more. And being a whole year younger than the older boys, the ones I'd be going to secondary school with in September, already made me different. If I couldn't play my part in saving the village, it would be another reason for them not to hang out with me.

Grandad Barry dunked a wooden spoon into a vat of baked beans. He walked to the first boy in line, Jordan, who wolfed the beans down in one. Jordan belched loudly. Grandad Barry nodded his approval.

Simon clipped on his nose peg and worked his way down the line of my belching schoolmates, decibel-reader in hand. Fuelled by spoonfuls of beans, each boy took it in turns to burp as loudly as they could. Their mums looked on from the sidelines and the boys grinned as they belched – all these beans, and their mums were *encouraging* them to burp!

The last boy in line was Martin. Asthmatic, weak-wristed Martin. I didn't hold out much hope. Grandad Barry held aloft a spoonful of beans and Martin grimaced at the thought of eating them cold. He held his nose and took the spoon. Slowly, so slowly – even slower than Dave, the absurdly old man – Martin opened his mouth and raised the spoon to his lips.

And then he fainted, flat out on the floor.

Grandad Barry and Simon rallied round him and sat him up. After a moment Martin opened his eyes. 'I can't do it,' he said sadly. 'I'm sorry.'

I wrung my hands in anguish from behind the bouncy castle. I wanted to reach out and help, but Mum was still marching around the green. She shuddered as a couple of Labradors from the dog stand shook themselves over her. I was too anxious to laugh.

'That's OK,' Simon said to Martin. 'It's not for everyone.'

The other boys in the line looked at Simon. 'Did we do it?' Jordan asked. 'Did we break the record?'

Simon peered at his decibel-reader and shook his head. 'Sorry. None of you were loud enough.'

The boys all stared at the ground in despair. 'I really wanted to break a record,' Martin whispered, and hung his head. 'I don't want to have to move from the village.'

Simon gave him a sad smile, but there was nothing he could do.

'And I wanted to help Luke's dad,' Martin said softly. 'I know what it's like to have a dad that's far away.'

I clapped my hand over my mouth. I hadn't realized Martin had cared. I didn't think any of my classmates did.

That was it. I glanced at Mum and saw that she was deep in conversation with Gwyn, so I seized the opportunity.

The boys stared at me as I pounded over to them, breathless. I'd forgotten I was wearing my disguise. 'It's me,' I said, lifting my glasses. 'I just wanted to say . . . to say . . .'

I wasn't sure *what* I wanted to say, but I knew I had to say something. I had to rally the troops. Then I remembered what Simon had said. 'You can do it,' I urged, trying to keep my voice steady. 'I know you can. We can all be record breakers, any one of us. If you want to be the best, and if you want to beat the rest, you just have to try. It might not happen the first time, but if you keep trying, you'll do it. Because you have to. For the village. To save our school and our houses and our mum and dad's jobs.'

I held out my hand to Martin. He smiled at me and took it. I lifted him to his feet and patted his shoulder.

Spurred on by my words, Martin grabbed the spoon from Grandad Barry and shovelled a massive spoonful of beans into his mouth. He chewed them slowly, his eyes widening at the taste. Then he gulped them down with purpose and took a deep breath. He opened his mouth wide, and burped.

It was a good belch. Clear, crisp and short.

But it wasn't loud enough. Simon checked his decibel-reader and frowned. 'Nope,' he said. Martin looked crushed. He'd been so convinced by my stirring words.

As if things weren't bad enough, Tim walked over to us.

He sidled up to me and hissed in my ear, 'Your turn now, Luke. Let's see what you can do.'

I didn't look at him. 'I'm not allowed to get involved,' I said quietly.

'What, your mum won't let you?' Tim said, and laughed cruelly. 'That's classic!' He could hardly contain his excitement.

Inside my head, I kicked myself that I'd given Tim the ammunition to laugh at me. I knew I had to act, and act fast. I made sure Mum couldn't see and then I shovelled a spoonful of beans into my mouth. I swallowed hard and tried to burp. Nothing came out. *Come on*, I thought to myself. *How many times had Mum given me one of her* Don't be disgusting *looks for burping in public and now I couldn't when I needed to?* I tried again. Still nothing, except this time I thought I was going to be sick. I couldn't see Tim's face, but I could tell he was laughing at me. I had failed again.

'It's OK,' Simon said softly. 'Burping's just not your thing.'

Tim laughed. 'Or cup stacking. What is?'

I didn't have anything to reply, because Tim was right. I was humiliated once more, right in front of my classmates.

Just then, Martin stepped out of the line. He walked over to Tim and clutched his stomach tightly. He slowly opened his mouth and looked like he was going to throw up, but instead he blasted out the most ear-splitting burp known to man. *BUUUUUUURRRPP!* A car alarm went off in the distance. Simon's decibel-reader flew off the chart.

Wow! I looked at Martin with new-found respect – he might have weak wrists, but his lungs were wonderful. I high-fived Martin in celebration, whilst the rest of the boys cheered.

Tim looked at all of us in disgust. 'Losers,' he blurted. 'All of you.'

'Technically not, actually,' Simon replied, and shook his decibel-reader. 'That was Port Bren's third successful record-breaking attempt.' Tim skulked away, for once defeated. This was ace!

Simon placed a hand on my shoulder and checked no one else could hear. 'You shouldn't let him get to you,' he whispered.

I didn't say anything. I couldn't believe Simon had spotted how much Tim annoyed me. I always thought I'd been pretty good at hiding it.

'You know, when I was your age,' Simon continued, 'a boy at my school used to tease—'

'It's none of your business,' I interrupted. I felt a bit mean – I knew Simon had only been trying to help, but I couldn't bear him trying to talk to me about it. The sort of talk that Dad would have given me.

I shrugged Simon's hand from my shoulder. 'Mum's coming,' I said, even though I had no idea where she was at that precise moment. I ran off before Simon could see that I'd started to cry.

I ducked out of sight behind the bouncy castle and wiped my eyes. Why did Tim always have to have a go at me?

A rustling sound behind me interrupted my thoughts. I crawled on my hands and knees to have a look and peeked round the corner.

Michael knelt down to the extension lead, where the motor fan that powered the castle was plugged in. He glanced about him and then pulled out the plug. Michael smiled as the motor fan slowed down, eventually stopping altogether.

Without any power, the castle quickly began to deflate. The elderly residents shrieked in panic as it collapsed in on them, the yellow turrets folding like a pack of cards. Villagers lay in a heap at the bottom, unable to get up. Dave, the absurdly old man, was winded by Glyn's flying walking stick, his painfully slow journey to reach Simon set back a couple of steps.

Michael swerved to avoid Absurdly Old Dave and accidentally banged into the dog post. The wooden stand collapsed under his weight. I expected Michael to look a bit shocked at this, but instead he just smiled as all the dogs started to shake themselves free. Perhaps Michael found it funny, though it wasn't, because all hell broke loose. All forty-seven dogs started to shake themselves over the villagers.

The men with frying pans were knocked off their unicycles as sheepdogs and poodles and bulldogs and terriers bounded over to them. Pancakes landed on the dart players' faces just as they were about to throw. Villagers ducked as darts soared haphazardly through the air. Dave, the absurdly old man, had just managed to get back on his feet and was about to set off towards Simon once more, when a roaming pug knocked him back down again.

'Keep going, everyone!' I yelled out amid the mayhem. I tried to encourage the village as devastation unfolded. I helped the dazed, confused and defeated villagers to their feet, but I couldn't rally them.

I saw Michael smiling amongst the chaos, so I ran over to him. 'What did you do to the bouncy castle?' I asked.

Michael looked down on me curiously, taking in my wig and glasses. 'I don't know what you're talking about, man,' he replied with a blank look.

'You took the plug out,' I said. 'And the castle collapsed.'

'If you knew, why did you ask me?' was all he came back with. He was about to walk off, when Grandad Barry

109

sidled up to me. 'What was that?' he asked.

I hesitated. Mum always said it wasn't nice to tell on people, but Michael had caused so much panic.

'Michael pulled the plug out?' Grandad Barry asked me, clearly having overheard anyway.

I nodded.

Michael frowned at me, but then looked Grandad Barry straight in the eye. 'I had to,' he replied. 'The motor fan was overheating. The whole thing could have gone up in flames.'

Grandad Barry didn't say anything for a moment, but then he beamed and slapped Michael on the back. 'Well done,' he boomed and motioned to the chaos around us. 'This is nothing compared to what a fire would have done. You're a real hero.'

Michael smiled at me as Grandad Barry jogged off. But before I could say anything, from the corner of my eye I saw Tim do the strangest thing. He picked up Sir Walter's glass case from the side of the green, walked towards Gareth's bathtub and opened the lid of the case, just a crack. Tim took a deep breath and then he shook the spider into Gareth's bath! He dropped the case and ran off, repeatedly wiping his hands on his trousers.

Gareth started to scratch his leg as if he felt an itch on it. He looked down and saw the tarantula inching its way up his thigh. At the sight of the spider, the blood drained from Gareth's face and he let out the loudest scream ever. *EVER!* Everyone on the green stopped what they were doing and stood in silence as it reverberated around us.

Simon walked over to Gareth, decibel-reader in hand. 'First loudest burp, now loudest scream,' he laughed as he scooped up Sir Walter from the bath. 'Anything else?'

The villagers cheered at this unexpected result. I don't know why Tim did what he did, but another record had been broken – and we hadn't even tried! Maybe Tim *wanted* us to succeed, though he had a funny way of showing it.

I looked at Michael again and this time noticed that he seemed distinctly unhappy with the village's unexpected success. Perhaps he hated loud noises, I thought. Though maybe now would be a good time to ask Michael about what I'd seen in the study. 'What do deeds mean?'

Michael didn't pay any attention and instead scowled at the villagers. 'Michael,' I said, a little louder this time. 'What do *deeds* mean?'

Grandad Barry accidentally banged into Michael as he hurried to slap a PASS sticker on Gwyn's chest. 'Ow!' Michael rubbed his elbow. He turned and looked down on me, his face like thunder. He must have got the look from Mum. 'Find it in the dictionary,' he growled, and stormed off.

111

Charming!

I shrugged and moved to the edge of the green, where the whole village had gathered to watch Jimmy's mum pile the last of the T-shirts on him. Jimmy's head was barely visible under the mound, and the sheer volume of T-shirts made him look like a giant marshmallow-man. 'Are you all right in there?' his mother asked in concern.

Jimmy managed to waggle his finger through the arm hole. 'My feet are a bit numb,' he called out in a muffled voice. I rolled my eyes – his feet had nothing to do with it.

'You're wearing one hundred and fifty T-shirts,' Simon counted in amazement. 'You've done it!'

Glyn enthusiastically slapped a PASS sticker on Jimmy's chest. The force tipped Jimmy and he fell off his stool in shock. He rolled over and over on the grass and, like a ladybird that's fallen on its back, he lay there flapping his legs in the air, unable to get up.

After what felt like an eternity, Dave, the absurdly old man, finally made it over to Simon and handed him the piece of paper he'd been clutching. It was his birth certificate.

Simon took in the details. 'You're one hundred and thirty?' he asked in astonishment.

Dave nodded. 'The Queen's stopped sending me birthday cards,' he sighed. 'Says I'm a fortune in stamps.'

Blimey. Older than Jeanne Calment, the French woman? Who'd have thought it!

'That's a new world record!' Simon grinned.

Just at that moment Victoria gave an almighty grunt and flung her baton up into the air, higher than it had ever twirled before. The crowd gasped as the baton flew all the way up and over the chart, breaking the record further than we could ever know. Victoria beamed as the crowd cheered and Glyn handed her a PASS sticker.

'That's all very well,' Grandad Barry said, 'but what goes up, must come down,' and villagers scattered as the baton came crashing to the ground. Except Dave, who was too exhausted from avoiding flying darts and roaming sheep-dogs and stood rooted to the spot. The baton struck him right on the crown and he promptly collapsed.

I took the PASS stickers from Glyn and slapped one on Dave's chest. Dave gave me a feeble thumbs-up to show that he was all right, if a little winded and dazed.

'Seven records broken!' I shouted wildly. 'Forty-three records to go.' The villagers cheered again. We were back on track.

I ducked out of sight as Mum marched over to find out what all the fuss was about. Grandad Barry squeezed her in celebration. 'We're on a roll, love,' he said. Mum smiled tightly. 'I'm going to start on my cake,' she said. 'Luke's back at the house, isn't he?'

Great, I thought. *Fun spoiled again*. I ran off the green, picked up my BMX and pedalled back to the house, keen to get there before Mum realized I'd gone.

Chapter Ten

I shoved my disguise under the bed, pulled my dictionary from my desk drawer and flicked through the pages. I stopped when I got to the word *Deeds*.

This is what it said:

1. Things consciously done. Brave, skilful or conspicuous act. Actual fact. Performance (kind in word and deed).

2. A document, affecting legal transfer of ownership and bearing disposer's signature.

'That's my good deed for the day,' Grandad Barry always said when he gave Gwyn a hand with her bags from his shop.

So Michael had been telling the truth about the castle – he'd done a good deed by not letting it overheat. But for some reason, it just didn't feel right.

I heard the front door slam. 'Luke?' Mum called from downstairs. I shoved the dictionary back in the drawer, before I even had the chance to look up *Ostentatious*.

In the kitchen, Mum had assembled a variety of food colourings, vegetables and ingredients on the worktop. She smiled as I entered and read from a home-made recipe book. 'Do you think the council will prefer Marmite delight, crème de cauliflower, or strawberry supreme for their cakes?' Mum asked.

I was lost in my own thoughts, still pondering what I'd seen in Michael's study, coupled with his strange behaviour on the green. I did a double take.

'Strawberry supreme?' I questioned as I finally registered what Mum had asked. That sounded far too normal for her.

Mum peered closer at her recipe book. 'Oh, no,' she replied. 'Couldn't read my own writing. It's *straw* supreme.' Mum began to hum as she took out pots and pans from the cupboards.

'Do you think anyone would want the village to fail, Mum?' I asked after a moment.

Mum raised her eyebrows in surprise. 'What makes you say that?'

I shrugged. 'Just something I saw, that's all.'

'What?' Mum asked. She cracked a couple of eggs into the cake bowl. 'Where?'

I was about to mention Michael and the bouncy castle, but then remembered I wasn't meant to have been there. If

I confided in Mum about witnessing Michael's actions on the green I would incriminate myself for directly disobeying her. And that would have been a whole other headache. 'Nothing,' I sighed. 'Don't worry.'

Mum passed me the bowl and I began to whisk the cake mix. A gloopy blend of eggs, flour, milk and tomato ketchup swirled round.

'Looking forward to dinner at Michael's?' Mum asked after a moment.

I shrugged again. 'S'pose.'

'He's nice once you get to know him.'

Mum put down her cake bowl and took me by the shoulders. She spun me round to face her and I could see that she was worried. 'I want you to *try* and like him,' she said, biting her lip. 'Because he's my boyfriend now.'

'He's not *my* boyfriend,' I muttered, but I didn't mean it like that.

'Don't you want me to be happy?' Mum asked. And then she added, 'You're not the only one who lost him, you know.'

I shoved the cake bowl on the counter. I had to get out of there.

'Wait,' Mum said, and she held me still. 'I'm sorry. I know you miss your dad. But it's been over a year, Luke. He's not coming back.' She studied my face. 'You do know that, don't you?'

117

I wanted to shout then. Loudly. At Mum, at the village, at anyone who would listen. I KNOW HE'S NOT COMING BACK! I wanted to yell. BUT THAT DOESN'T STOP ME WISHING HE WOULD!

But I didn't say anything.

As dinner time approached, I rang the doorbell of Michael's mansion. After a moment the door opened. This was the bit I'd been dreading.

'Uncle Michael's in the front room,' Tim said and held the door open for us. I looked down at my feet as we piled inside. When no one was looking, Tim flicked the back of my head as he showed us into the front room. I grimaced and tried to pretend I wasn't bothered.

Michael's front room was as posh as the rest of his house and as big as the whole of the downstairs of Grandad Barry's put together. Plush cream leather sofas filled the room; Michael had every modern gadget under the sun, with his 80-inch plasma-screen telly taking up the whole of the back wall. A glass cabinet sprawled the length of one side of the room and contained hundreds of framed photos. They must have been taken by the same rubbish photographer, though, because they were all blurred or out of focus. Every one of them was of Michael doing the most adventurous things he could – skydiving out of a plane;

118

water skiing in the Pacific Ocean. 'Not one to hide his light under a bushel,' Grandad Barry whispered to me.

We all sat in the front room, no one quite knowing what to say. It got a bit boring after a while – all I wanted to do was ask Simon about the record attempts.

'The record attempts are going well,' Simon said eventually. I couldn't believe it! It was as if he'd read my mind.

I was about to start grilling him when Michael clicked his fingers. 'Enough about records,' he boomed. 'Luke's surprise is better than records.'

Hold on a second, I thought. *Nothing is better than records. Except maybe chocolate ice cream.*

Michael's housekeeper, Doris, stepped into the room, holding a baby gecko.

'Wow!' I said in amazement. Thinking about it, a gecko came a close second.

'What?!' Tim said in disbelief. 'How come he gets a present?' He scowled. 'And where's my tenner? From the green?'

Michael narrowed his eyes at Tim as Doris held the gecko out to me. But rather than take it, I held back. 'Um, it's really cool, and everything,' I said, and just patted the gecko, 'but I'd quite like a tarantula now.' And one tarantula in particular. I'd been enchanted by Sir Walter ever since

Simon had come to Port Bren and, as well as thinking about how to save the village, I'd been trying to think of ways I could make Simon 'forget' to take Sir Walter home with him.

Simon opened his suit pocket. In it, Sir Walter was nestled, asleep. 'He goes everywhere with me.' Simon smiled. Out of the corner of my eye I watched as Tim slowly sidled away from Simon, his eyes wider than I'd ever seen them.

Michael frowned at me. 'You won't be fussed about the spider when you've got used to the gecko, that's for sure.'

Mum gave me a Look, suggesting I should at least try to like it and show some sort of gratitude for Michael's present, so I picked up the gecko and stroked him again. 'I'll call him Sir Winston,' I announced. 'After Churchill.'

Mum tapped Michael softly on the wrist. 'You'll spoil him,' she scolded. 'Scott never did. He always said it would turn him soft.'

'That's because Scott never had the money to,' Michael replied. He could be a bit flash at times, Michael could.

Mum looked a bit put out by his comment, but before she could reply Simon stood up, desperate to leave the awkwardness. 'Where's the bathroom?' he asked.

'Which one?' Michael boasted. He could be *very* flash at times. 'First floor,' he added after a blank reaction from Simon.

I thought for a second. I hadn't had the chance to ask Mum about Michael's behaviour, so perhaps Simon could help. Offer impartial advice, maybe. I leaped up from the sofa, scooping Sir Winston under my arm. 'I, uh, need to go too,' I said quickly.

'Use the one on the fourth floor,' Michael said. He had five floors, you see. Grandad Barry always said that *we* could have had five floors, but it would take him all week to clean. And I know for a fact that he didn't have a special-occasion toupee for that.

I caught up with Simon in the corridor and motioned upstairs. 'I need to show you something,' I whispered. Simon followed me up the stairs and down the oak-panelled hallway of the fourth floor.

When we got to the study, I looked around to check no one could see, and then opened the door. 'Promise you won't say anything?' I asked. 'It's important.'

Simon nodded and I scooted over to the desk in the corner. I plonked Sir Winston down on top of the desk and started rifling about. 'What are you doing?' Simon asked nervously from the doorway.

'I saw a piece of paper here, before,' I replied. 'It said *Deeds to the land*, and it had Michael's signature under-neath.'

A full minute of silence passed. I looked back at Simon

and saw that he had a funny expression on his face. 'Simon?'

'Are you sure that's what it said?' he asked.

I nodded.

'Right,' he replied slowly. 'Can you remember where you saw it?'

I motioned to the desk. Simon scooted into the room, joining me in rifling through the numerous pieces of paper scattered on the desk top.

'I can't find it,' I said after a moment. 'Michael must have moved it somewhere.'

Simon was one step ahead and had started searching through all the bookshelves. I joined him, feeling along the tops of all the books.

Just then, Simon started to sniff. I did too. An unpleasant, yet not unfamiliar, smell filled our nostrils. 'Sir Winston?' Simon whispered. The gecko wasn't on the desk. Simon bent down to the source of the smell – an open desk drawer. He reached inside and pulled out a soggy piece of paper. Simon flapped it in the air. 'No wonder your Grandad didn't want you to have one,' he said, unimpressed by Sir Winston's visit to the toilet. I stifled a laugh.

Simon extracted a wet wipe from his pocket and brushed it lightly over the paperwork. The ink started to run.

'Oh, God,' Simon said, panicked. He tried again, but still the ink ran. Not knowing what else to do, he wiped the paper on his suit jacket instead. He shuddered in disgust and nearly gagged. I couldn't help but laugh out loud. 'I'm glad you find this funny,' Simon said.

He looked closely at the paper to see if Sir Winston's wee stain had gone and, as he read what was on it, his face changed. 'Bingo!' he whispered after a while.

He held out the paper to me. 'Was this it?' I recognized the official-looking stamp. Three curling green leaves in the corner.

The door handle rattled. Simon motioned for me to be quiet. He checked all around the desk for the gecko. 'Sir Winston?' he hissed. The door handle rattled again and Simon and I turned to face it in dread. Panicked, Simon gritted his teeth and stuffed the wee-stained paperwork down his trousers. The door opened slowly, and Doris entered the room.

She was clearly startled by our presence. 'Does Mr Harding know you're in here?' she enquired, pursing her lips together. Neither I nor Simon knew what to say. 'Or perhaps I should go and ask him?'

Simon cleared his throat. He wiped a finger along one of the bookshelves, then inspected it and showed his finger to Doris. There was nothing on it. 'Going for world's dustiest

123

house, are we?' Simon stuttered, trying to bluff his way out of our snooping.

Doris looked like she'd swallowed a lemon, but pulled a duster from her pinny and stormed around the study, cleaning like there was no tomorrow. Simon cringed with guilt.

I motioned wildly to him, flailing my arms around. I'd found Sir Winston. Trouble was, he was nestled on top of the door frame, about to launch himself at Doris's head!

Simon sighed and crept over to Doris. He slowly raised his arms. Then, in one swift move, he scooped the gecko off the door and cupped him in his hands. We ran for the exit.

'Sorry!' I shouted back at Doris as I slammed the door shut.

Simon let out a big puff of air as he leaned against the oak-panelled wall and passed Sir Winston back to me. 'That was close,' he panted.

And then it all clicked into place. I finally understood what was going on. A light bulb switched on above my head.

'Sorry about that,' Simon said, and leaned away from the light switch.

'Dead Glyn didn't sell his land, did he?' I whispered.

Simon shook his head and pointed to his trousers. 'Not

if this is anything to go by.' He meant the paperwork, not his trousers. 'It's Michael's signature on the contract,' he explained. 'Dead Glyn left Michael the farmland in his will and then Michael sold it to the waste plant.'

'That's why he unplugged the bouncy castle,' I said. A look of surprise crossed Simon's face. 'On the green, this afternoon. I saw him.'

My mind whirred as I tried to make sense of everything. 'Michael wasn't trying to be a hero,' I whispered. 'He *wants* us to fail.' I thought back to Tim on the green too. 'And he must have promised Tim money to scare Gareth in the bath. With Sir Walter. Tim was after his tenner when we got here.'

Simon smiled at me. 'A right little Sherlock, aren't you?'

I shook my head in frustration. 'But why would Michael sell the land?'

Simon shrugged. 'Money, probably. An awful lot of it. It's funny, though. Him telling you to look it up in the dictionary has ultimately led to his downfall.'

It didn't seem particularly funny to me.

'What about *us*?' I asked Simon eventually. 'What about my dad?' I couldn't believe it – Michael had used Dad's *World's Best Dad* mug! That was it – I was going to give Michael a piece of my mind. And not a very nice piece, either.

I started to race off along the corridor, but Simon held me back by my T-shirt. 'Whoa there!' he called. 'Not so fast.'

'But we've got to tell him that we know,' I said. 'I've got to tell Mum what he's up to.'

'I don't think that's the way to play it,' Simon replied. 'At this moment in time, Michael thinks all he has to do is make sure the village doesn't succeed, then the plant gets built. He'll get his money.'

'So we have to stop him,' I cried.

Simon shook his head. 'If we *know* Michael's up to no good, we can keep tabs on him,' he said. 'Michael won't know that we're watching him, and when he does try and sabotage the record attempts, we'll be able to spot and stop him. But if Michael knows we're on to him, then there's no telling what he'll do. He could very well go behind our backs.'

That sort of made sense to me. 'We'll have the upper hand?' I asked.

'Precisely,' Simon replied.

I felt bad about lying to Mum, especially now I knew what a creep her new boyfriend was. But I had no choice – it was to save Dad. Just a little White Lie.

Simon took me by the elbow and led me back to the front room. He walked a little awkwardly because he still had the paperwork shoved down his trousers. 'I'm sorry about before,' he said softly. 'On the green. I didn't mean to lecture you.' He bit his lip. 'I wasn't trying to be your dad, or anything.'

I shrugged. 'It's OK,' I replied.

Simon nodded his gratitude. 'Well, in the meantime,' he said, as upbeat as he could manage, 'you'll have to do all you can to succeed.'

I looked a bit sad then, knowing that I couldn't help the villagers in their attempts. But Simon smiled kindly at me. 'I suggest you keep wearing your disguise,' he whispered, and winked.

As we got back into the front room, Michael sniffed the air, smelling the stench of wee. 'Are you sure you made it to the bathroom?' he asked Simon, pulling a face. Simon ignored him and motioned for me to sit.

I ran over to the sofa, sat down with Sir Winston and had to try very hard not to glare at Michael and give the game away.

Friday
Chapter Eleven

Fifty-one hours to save Port Bren. As dawn broke, I dragged my disguise out from under the bed and shoved it on quickly. I'd thought of something I could do to help the village, and no one even need know it was me. Ever so quietly I snuck out of my bedroom and padded downstairs.

From the front garden I picked up my BMX and pedalled off towards Mrs Wilson's house. The headmistress was surprised to see me, but she let me borrow a whiteboard from the school nonetheless.

'Anything to help us in our mission,' she trilled. 'You haven't heard from Mr Wilson, have you? I can't get hold of him.'

'He *is* in a canoe halfway out to sea,' I replied, leaning back on my BMX.

I set up the whiteboard in the middle of the green. On one side I wrote all the record attempts; on the other, their outcome. It looked like this:

1. Most doughnuts eaten in one minute – Trevor　　　　**Pass**

2. Most hula hoops hula-hooped in one minute – Gwyn   Pass

3. Longest continual chorus – Daffydd and the   Ongoing
   male choir

4. Most dogs washed in one hour – Port Bren Brownies   Fail

5. Most T-Shirts worn – Jimmy   Pass

And so on.

Gwyn had wanted a tally for the entire village to see, so that's what I did.

I hopped back on my bike and pedalled home, pleased I'd been able to at least play a small part.

On the way, I saw Walking-Stick Glyn outside Adam Leroux's farm. Glyn was ducking down by the rickety old side gate, clutching a whistle and a dog lead. He grinned when he saw me. 'Not giving up, son,' he said, and rose to his feet. 'Cover me, I'm going in.' Glyn looked both ways and then hoisted himself up onto the gate. It took three attempts and several buckets of sweat, but he managed to cling onto the top. The gate shook under his weight. Puffing and panting, and with his legs scrabbling underneath him, Glyn threw himself over the top, landing in a heap on the ground the other side. He leaped to his feet excitedly. 'Made it!' he cried. 'The SAS have nothing on me!'

I rolled my eyes and then stepped forward and undid the catch on the gate. It swung open with ease. 'Nobody likes a show-off,' Glyn muttered. He shuffled into the field and approached the nearest cow. In one fell swoop, he threw the dog lead around her neck and gently tried to coax the cow to follow him. 'Come here, Miribel,' Glyn cooed. 'Good cow.'

Miribel ignored him and continued grazing on the grass, her tail flicking every now and then to swat a fly. Glyn blew his whistle at her instead, but still the cow didn't move. I could have stayed all day to watch, it was that funny, but at that moment Simon came marching down the lane, leading a trail of villagers towards the high street. Striding along, with everyone walking single file behind him, Simon looked a bit like the Pied Piper. But without the rats. Or the tights.

They walked past Bill, the mechanic, as he tinkered under the bonnet of Simon's car. 'Soon be ready for you, Mr David,' Bill said. 'We'll get you back to London yet.'

I was a bit worried to hear that. As soon as Bill had fixed Simon's car and the record attempts were over, Simon would be off again, and that made me sad. I'd enjoyed having him in the village. In the house. It was nice to talk to someone about records. Someone who actually knew what they were talking about. Like Dad.

Simon spotted me, and he must have known exactly what I was thinking because he said, 'Don't worry. I'm not going anywhere just now.' I felt a bit better after that.

A gaggle of onlookers from Marvel Barton approached

us. I counted about thirty people – so *everyone* from Marvel Barton, then. Brenda, who was very pretty for an old woman and was training to be a belly dancer, waved to Grandad Barry. 'This waste plant's going to affect Marvel Barton too,' she called. 'We're here to support you.'

Grandad Barry nodded in delight and looked at Brenda appreciatively. Gwyn glared at Brenda's skimpy attire. 'That's all very well and good,' she scowled, 'but if Port Bren is to become truly famous, we'll need more than Marvel Barton.' She gave Brenda a tight smile. 'No offence.'

I thought for a moment. Make Port Bren famous. Now *that* I could do. I leaped back on my BMX.

Moments later I knocked on the door of the newspaper reporter's office. The 'office' being his house, where the *Jersey Journal* was written, edited and printed from his attic. It was hardly *The Times*.

The reporter swigged from his coffee cup and ushered me in. He cocked his head to one side as I breathlessly told him of our plans to save Port Bren. 'The village with the most records broken in the world!' I cried. 'No village has ever done that before.'

The newspaper reporter rolled his eyes. 'I can see where you get it from,' he said. 'How's your mum's protest coming along?'

'She's making the council a cake.'

The reporter laughed loudly. Clearly he'd heard of Mum's terrible baking.

'So will you write about it?' I asked. 'It's front-page news.'

Jersey Journal guy thought about it for a second and then shook his head. 'I don't think so.'

'What?' I cried out incredulously. 'It's the most exciting thing to happen to Jersey in ages. And it's got nothing to do with cows. Well, hardly anything.'

The reporter looked at his watch. 'Tell you what,' he said half-heartedly, clearly keen to get rid of me. 'I'll write an article. One article. I've probably got a bit of space by the obituaries.'

'Great,' I replied. 'Thanks for nothing.'

This was rubbish. If the council said Port Bren had to be put on the map in order to contest building of the waste plant, we'd need more than an article next to the obituary page in the *Jersey Journal* to do it.

We would need TV.

The idea came to me in a flash. *Why hadn't I thought of it before?* Think of all the record attempts I'd watched on the Internet or on DVD! TV would be just the thing! 'Fine,' I said to the reporter as he tried to usher me out the front door. 'I'll ask the BBC.'

The reporter stopped in his tracks. 'What?'

'We need to get famous somehow,' I replied. 'If you won't do it, I'll get the telly involved.'

Jersey Journal guy scratched his freckly chin as he looked me over. He could see that I was serious, but how could a little boy summon a TV crew to a tiny, backwater village? 'Good luck with that,' he snorted in derision. 'They'll never come.'

Four hours later the newspaper reporter was standing on the side of the village green, his mouth wide open in shock. 'How did you—?' he spluttered to me. I beamed at him behind my glasses as a white van parked on the middle of the green.

A man dressed in a suit and clutching a microphone jumped out of the van. A younger man with a nose stud and a clipboard followed. Behind them a woman in jeans and T-shirt hovered around, filming everything.

The TV reporter checked his notes, and then looked me up and down. He took in my toupee and oversized coat. 'Mr Scott Deeds?' he asked.

I had to bite my lip to stop myself laughing. 'That's me,' I said, under the disguise.

The TV reporter nodded to his crew. 'Port Bren, the village that, like a dying family dog, just won't be put down,' he said. He looked at his surroundings and spotted

Glyn wandering about clutching Miribel's dog lead. 'But is that a good thing?'

Grandad Barry extended his hand to the TV reporter. 'Six o'clock news, are you?' he boomed.

'*Look Jersey*,' the reporter replied. 'Not much difference.'

About eight million viewers difference, I thought. I'd tried to get BBC News involved, but the telephone operator I'd asked couldn't find the number. The telephone operator was Mrs Jenkins, who dressed up her cats as babies and took them for walks in prams, so I wasn't at all surprised. Still, after several phone calls and a few White Lies – and I mean *Serious* White Lies – I'd managed to persuade a TV crew to visit. I'd had to give a false name because Mum had been hovering just outside the kitchen while I made the phone call. Scott Deeds had been the first thing I'd thought of.

And yet they came. We were going to be famous. I had done *something* to help.

The TV reporter looked at his notes again and then turned to me. 'So, this "Balancing on a cow on a tightrope three hundred metres in the air" attempt is next, yes?' he checked.

I bit my lip again. Some *Serious* White Lies, indeed. 'Uh, not quite,' I replied, and motioned for the villagers to follow me.

I led everyone inside the B & B guesthouse on the high street, which was the venue for the next attempt. As we entered the hallway Anil, a mainlander from Leicester who had come to Mrs Renoir's B & B twelve years ago but had forgotten to check out, sat at the top of the stairs, his ample frame wedged into an inflatable dinghy. 'Ready when you are, Simon,' he shouted, shuffling on his bum to get into position.

'Uh, Anil?' Simon stuttered, confused. But Anil didn't hear him.

With a gleeful *'Wheeeeeeeeeeee!'* Anil launched himself down the stairs in an effort to break the 'Fastest time to race down thirteen stairs on an inflatable dinghy' record. Except he'd forgotten to inflate it.

Anil flew forward as the dinghy caught the top step and he came crashing down the stairs, hitting every single one on the way. He landed in an awkward heap at our feet and groaned.

'We'll come back,' Simon sighed, and led us all onwards.

Villagers and the camera crew crammed inside a tiny room only as big as my bedroom. Mrs Renoir, the landlady, insisted on calling it the 'Honeymoon Suite', as it was the most prestigious room in the B & B, though Mum had said it was only because guests received an extra mint on the pillow.

Simon held up his stopwatch as Mrs Renoir struggled inside a duvet cover, entangling herself further the more she struggled. She looked hopeless, but at least she was trying. After about forty seconds, she decided to give up. Which was just as well as the record for the fastest time to put on a duvet was 13.56 seconds. Mrs Renoir collapsed on the bed in a heap. Another fail.

I knew we weren't going to get anywhere at this rate – the TV crew wouldn't stick around if the village kept failing – and I threw my glasses on the floor in frustration, forgetting momentarily that I was meant to remain in disguise.

Mum, who had come to provide cake for the TV crew, gave me a strange look. 'I recognize that hairpiece,' she said, staring closely at my wig.

'Oh, come on,' I cried to Simon, ignoring Mum. 'We're so close.'

Simon shook his head. It was clear he wasn't going to budge on the matter.

So I tried a different tack. 'Don't do it for the village, then,' I said to Simon, 'do it for Mum, ah, Mrs Meldrum,' I corrected quickly. 'Grandad Barry, ah, I mean, Barry,' I corrected again – I wasn't great at this pretending lark – '*Barry* says you fancy her.' I knew I'd gone too far, but I *had* to save the village.

Grandad Barry laughed as Simon blushed and

confirmed my observation, and the villagers murmured in delight. Mum folded her arms to show she was not impressed and she fixed me with a piercing stare.

Simon attempted to regain control of the situation, pushing the news camera out of his face. 'No,' he said firmly. 'Sorry.'

I huffed and stormed off. I didn't want to witness another fail.

Annoyed that things weren't going to plan, I rode around the village on my BMX, not sure where I was heading. As I cycled down the village high street, I almost flew headfirst over my handlebars – I hadn't seen the wooden ramp positioned in front of the library.

'Watch out!' a voice cried behind me. Then Owen whizzed past me on his black mountain bike and rode up the wooden ramp. He then launched off and soared into the distance. He landed the bike expertly and the tyres screeched as he came to a stop.

Izzy paced towards Owen, placing one foot in front of another, counting all the while to herself. 'Two hundred and six feet!' she shouted in amazement, when she finally reached Owen's bike. I rolled my eyes at Izzy's haphazard measuring system.

Owen saw me. I turned my bike round, ready to peg it, but he blocked my path. 'Got a problem?' he demanded.

I shook my head and got ready to pedal. 'Then what's with you pulling faces at my sister?'

'I didn't!' I replied, but Owen looked like he wanted to punch me. So I reached into my pocket and took out one of Simon's spare tape measures. 'You might find it easier to measure with this,' I said.

Owen peered at me and then snatched the tape measure from my hand. He looked me up and down. 'Think I'll break a record?' he asked, and then he smiled. *He smiled at me.*

'I – uh,' I said, completely taken by surprise. Owen had never, ever been *nice* to me. I was more surprised than if I'd been told an alien had been found in the foliage round the back of Grandad Barry's shop. Actually, an alien *had* once been found in the foliage round the back of Grandad Barry's shop, but it turned out it was just a fancy-dress costume.

'I think you'll need a few more metres,' I managed to stutter. 'The current record for the world's longest bike jump is eighty-four point seven, I think.'

Owen and Izzy looked a bit downcast at that, but I didn't want this period of – well, not *friendship*, exactly, but whatever you'd call not being beaten up – to end, so I quickly added, 'But I reckon you could do it.'

Izzy beamed right at me, whilst Owen replied, 'Yeah, I

reckon.' He shrugged his shoulders casually, but I could tell he was dead chuffed.

Then Tim turned up, and everything went back to how it always was. 'What's all this?' he demanded. He'd put in some of his freaky contact lenses, so his eyes flashed red as he took in the wooden ramp, and me and Owen chatting. 'Don't tell me you're joining in with this geek?'

He noticed the tape measure in Owen's hand. 'That yours?' He frowned.

Owen quickly shook his head and thrust the tape measure back at me. Tim laughed. 'Might have guessed.'

Before I could do anything, Tim yanked the tape measure from me and took a penknife from his pocket. He flicked the knife open, and, in one swift move, cut the tape measure clean in two. Owen looked a bit shocked, but he quickly covered it up. 'I don't care what you do with his stupid tape measure,' he said, not quite able to meet my gaze.

'Good,' Tim replied. He let the two halves of the tape measure flutter to the ground, then motioned for Owen and Izzy to follow him. I didn't hang around and pedalled off back down the high street as quickly as I could.

I found myself at Dad's grave. Truth was, I always found myself at Dad's grave. Whenever I was sad, whenever things went wrong. Apart from my birthday, I hardly ever came to see him with good things. I told him how the village was getting on with the attempts – some good, some bad, but how all of us were trying to pull together. Well, almost all of us. I told Dad how I'd sort of nearly bonded with Owen until Tim had turned up. 'It's not fair,' I muttered to him. 'He always spoils everything. I hate him.'

I kicked at the grass beneath my feet in frustration. Sometimes I wished Dad could reply. He'd tell me everything would be OK. How we'd break all the records and how Tim would stop punching me whenever he wanted. But then I remembered what Dad had always said when I said *It's not fair*. 'No,' he would reply. 'It's not fair until March. That's when spring starts,' and then he'd laugh his head off, which was so annoying.

I'd give anything for him to say it now, though.

I let out a big sigh. 'Why did you have to die?' I whispered softly. It really wasn't fair.

In our kitchen later that evening, Simon let me handle Sir Walter. I think he felt bad about what had happened in the B & B and, even though I was still annoyed with him, I wasn't going to say no. It was practically the only thing Mum would let me do.

Simon placed his hand inside Sir Walter's enclosure and gently guided the spider onto his palm. 'It's OK,' he whispered to him in a soothing voice. 'You're among friends.' Simon let Sir Walter walk onto his hand and then he held him out to me. 'He won't bite,' he laughed. 'He's probably more afraid of you than you are of him.'

I took Sir Walter and gently held him in the palm of my hand. The spider didn't move, so I stroked him on his back, ever so gently. He seemed to like that – one of his legs twitched in recognition. I smiled. Sure, having a gecko in a tank in your mum's creepy boyfriend's house was OK, but seriously, how brilliant was a real, live, twitching tarantula?

'They're naturally shy creatures,' Simon said in a voice that was slightly higher than normal. He pulled at his tie, and looked over to where Mum was cleaning the oven. 'But they like to feel loved every now and then.'

The phone rang. 'Have any of the other people trying to break records ever held Sir Walter?' I asked, trying to sound casual. I quite liked the thought of it being something that just Simon and I did. I imagined that all over the world Simon had made friends with lots of potential record breakers, so I wouldn't be anything special, and I didn't like that. I liked Simon being in *my* house, helping *my* village, with me being his best friend and all-round-most-knowledgeable-person-about-records-ever in Port Bren.

Before Simon could reply, Mum thrust the phone into his hand. She mouthed the word *MAX!* at him.

Simon cleared his throat and gulped nervously. 'Good evening, sir,' he said into the phone.

'There's my boy,' Max boomed back at him, so loudly I could hear everything. Max had a voice to rival Grandad Barry's, that was for sure. 'Good stuff, Simon. Good stuff indeed.'

Simon wiped his forehead. 'Thank you, sir,' he stuttered.

'Just wanted to touch base,' Max continued. 'Everything all right there?'

Simon looked round at us, his hosts. I held up Sir Walter to Mum, but she squirmed away in disgust. She didn't mind really, though, because she was smiling. I think she was just glad I was doing something that wasn't records. 'Everything's great, sir,' Simon replied into the phone.

'Good,' Max chuckled back to him. 'You keep this up, Simon, and it'll be you flying out to Australia for that promotion.'

Simon beamed with joy. It was the biggest smile he had smiled since he arrived in Port Bren, and something about it made me smile right back.

But thanks to Michael, it didn't last long.

Saturday
Chapter Twelve

With barely twenty-four hours to save Port Bren, Simon, Mum and a band of villagers surveyed the village green. In my disguise, I hid at the back of the crowd. A few hours earlier the green had been the hub of our operation; centre point of all things records. Now it had been completely swamped by building materials.

Wooden crates stacked full of breeze blocks, and bags of sand and cement were piled in rows. Cranes, fork-lift trucks and diggers lined the edges of the green. There was no room to move. My whiteboard lay on the ground, battered. The results so far – of twenty-nine passes, seven fails – were barely visible. The TV reporter instructed his crew to film this disappointing setback.

Michael picked his way through the rubble to join us. 'This is outrageous!' he said, clambering over several crates to get to the front of the crowd. 'How on earth can anyone get anything done with all this going on?'

Simon glared at him. *Of course*, I thought, *this was all down to him*. We hadn't seen this one coming.

Simon cleared his throat. 'Uh, there's something you should know,' he stuttered to the villagers, seemingly ready to reveal all. But before he could elaborate, he was interrupted by Grandad Barry, who lumbered onto the green wearing a string vest and shorts, and boxing gloves on his hands.

'We can't stop,' Grandad Barry thundered as he took in the building materials and the dejected look on the faces of the villagers before him. 'We can't be defeated.'

Michael tried to rally the crowd. 'Too right,' he said. 'We're not going down without a fight. Determination's what you need, isn't it? If you want to be a record breaker?'

I rolled my eyes at Michael's mistake. Simon did the same. 'It's *dedication*,' Simon and I said in unison.

I saw Mum look closely at the small boy before her in the wig and glasses.

Simon tried to say something more. 'Uh, it's about the land.' He pulled at his tie. 'I was just wondering what happens if you do fail?'

Grandad Barry frowned. 'Thanks for the optimism, Simon.'

Simon held up his hands in protest. 'No, no, I'm sure you won't,' he replied. 'But what if things conspired to stop you breaking fifty records?'

'What things?' Grandad Barry asked. I wasn't sure where Simon was going with this.

'Oh, you know. Things like this – the building materials. Things like . . . people.'

Michael raised an eyebrow. 'People?' he asked, and looked directly at Simon.

'Are you mad?' Grandad Barry boomed. 'Everyone wants to succeed. Those who've taken the money have taken the money. The rest of us, we're fighting to keep our homes by doing all the records. And that has to work, because we haven't got a plan B.'

'The very creation of a plan B means you're accepting failure,' I said quietly. I stared at the ground and willed myself not to cry as I spoke. 'You're accepting a second choice before you've even tried to achieve your first.'

Simon was taken aback. 'Blimey,' he said. 'Where did that come from?'

Mum walked over towards me. I gulped. I knew that by saying what I had, I'd given the game away. I hadn't even thought about it, I'd said it so instinctively.

Mum pulled down my glasses and peeled off my coat and special-occasion toupee (quiz nights). Jimmy and a few of the villagers gasped in surprise as I was unmasked.

I waited for Mum to shout and yell and tell me off for joining in with the record attempts and going against her

145

wishes, but she didn't. 'Your father used to make that very same speech,' she said softly. 'And now that's enough of records. The glasses and Dad's coat didn't fool me for one second, but I let you run around and have your fun. Now things are getting too serious – so, come on, home we go.'

I hung my head and started to slink off, defeated once more.

But then Simon called me back. 'Wait a second,' he cried. 'Luke should be here for this.'

Mum looked on curiously as Simon turned to the villagers. 'It's time you all knew the truth—'

But before he could get any further, he was interrupted once again. An excited squeal rang from the back of the crowd and drowned Simon out.

A family came running over the green towards the villagers. The mum, dad and two daughters, who looked to be about my age, ran at me, weaving in and out of sandbags and breeze blocks. The mum reached forward and grabbed me by the shoulders – she was freakishly strong – and pulled me to her, whilst the father got out a digital camera and started clicking away. The daughters stood on either side of me, striking a number of camera poses.

'What're you doing?' I managed to shout as soon as I could take a breath.

The father paused from his photographic duties. 'This is

Port Bren, *ja*?' he asked in a strong German accent. 'We watch on the TV all the records.'

Everyone turned to see what looked like an army of tourists march towards us. They streamed across the rickety old bridge that hung over the small stone quarry at the entrance to Port Bren, and snaked into the village like a line of ants. Some were carrying suitcases, some were snapping away on cameras. A little girl cartwheeled her way over.

That changed things somewhat.

'Oh. My. God!' I yelled. 'Mainlanders!' Everyone was too excited to spit.

The TV reporter perked up at the sheer volume of newcomers. 'It's made the national news?' he asked the German family in surprise.

Michael scowled at all the impending arrivals, which made Simon and me smile. Clearly he hadn't been expecting anything like this. No one had. The villagers started chatting animatedly at the sight of the tourists.

'People!' Gwyn exclaimed as if she'd never seen other human beings before. 'Don't they look wonderful!'

Glyn leaned on his walking stick in shock. 'We're really doing it!' he cried breathlessly. 'Port Bren's becoming famous!'

And just like that, a new sense of hope began to rise. Everyone forgot about the materials that swamped the green and renewed their determination to succeed in saving the village.

With all the extra people, spectators and curious bods coming to see Port Bren fight back, Grandad Barry suggested we do the right thing and open our homes to them all. 'For a small fee.' He winked.

News had spread of our multiple record attempts, and all these tourists wanted in on the action. Port Bren's only ferry had never seen so much action. Though considering it usually only ferried four people and the occasional cow, this wasn't hard. Cars were parked, suitcases were handed over, arms were welcoming.

Grandad Barry placed a small sign in the window of the front room, with *B & D* written on it.

Walking-Stick Glyn leaned in to read it. 'Don't you mean B and B?' he asked.

'Bed and Dinner, my friend,' Grandad Barry replied. 'Bed and Dinner. I'm finding the niche in the market, you see. I've seen *Dragon's Den*.'

An overweight, badly dressed tourist with non-matching socks handed Grandad Barry his suitcase. Grandad Barry smiled at him. 'Nice trip?' he asked. 'Where are you from?'

'Frome,' the tourist replied with a strong West Country accent.

'Sorry,' Grandad Barry apologized. 'Where are you frome?'

* * *

As Simon prepared to make his way back to the village green to continue with some more record attempts he decided to help me out. He approached Mum as we concocted another cake in the kitchen. I'd stacked all our previous efforts against the wall and formed a tower of eleven Marmite delights, crème de cauliflowers and straw supremes ready to send to the council.

Simon cleared his throat. 'Leek surprise?'

Mum huffed. 'I can do more than one flavour, thank you.'

'Yes, I know,' Simon replied. 'I just thought that was your signature dish.'

Mum looked him over, and I could tell she was wondering how he'd remembered a comment she'd made in passing, but I knew it was probably to do with what Grandad Barry said about Simon fancying her. 'It is,' she said, and tried hard to look annoyed. But I could tell that she really wanted to laugh. Mum had been really odd like that since Simon had come to stay – one minute she'd be all mad and cross about the records; the next, she'd be laughing her head off at something Simon had said to her.

Mum leaned over the counter top and reached for the salt shaker. Her arm brushed past several mugs she'd just washed up and they rattled about.

'Careful!' Simon cried, leaping forward to catch them before they fell.

Their hands touched as Mum bent to straighten the mugs. Mum jumped a little in shock, but she held onto his hand tightly. 'Dad's been promising for ages to make me a wooden mug tree,' she whispered breathlessly, her fingers still intertwined with Simon's.

'They're tricky things to make,' Simon whispered back, his voice seeming to stick in his throat. 'Has he thought about metal?'

They held each other's gaze. Now Simon was being all soppy and gross, but actually, I didn't mind it half as much as Mum and Michael. At least Simon wasn't a creep.

Still, it got a bit boring after a while. I coughed to break the silence. Simon jerked back and straightened his tie. 'Ah, yes,' he said, looking down at his clipboard. 'That was it. I'm finding all this quite difficult, you know, keeping tabs on the villagers, whilst helping them get organized for their attempts. I might need some assistance.'

Mum shrugged. 'You could phone your boss.'

'I meant Luke.'

I looked at Simon in delight, and he winked at me in return. *How ace!*

But then Mum's whole face changed and she went back to being annoyed. 'No,' she said firmly.

'What do you have against records?' Simon asked quietly.

Mum started whisking her cake mix vigorously. 'I'm busy,' she scowled.

'He would just be my assistant,' Simon ploughed on. 'I can't get involved with people in the village, so he would be my go-between.'

'Why do you care so much?' Mum snapped at him.

Simon shrugged. 'I don't like to see him unhappy,' he said softly. 'Do you?'

Mum gently put down the cake bowl. Just as she opened her mouth to reply, the doorbell rang.

It was Michael. I glowered as he came into the kitchen and gave Mum a peck on the cheek. I'd half a mind to reveal I knew everything, but Simon shook his head at me not to.

'Full house in here, isn't it?' Michael said playfully to Mum as he looked Simon up and down. 'Should I be worried about strange men living under your roof?'

'Simon's not strange,' I blurted out.

Michael laughed. 'Don't panic,' he said. 'I'm not really worried.'

He turned to Mum and ran his finger round the cake bowl. 'Straw supreme?' he asked as he licked the cake mix. 'Why don't you try it without the straw, sweetie?'

151

Mum took the bowl off him, and added more flour. 'It's leek surprise,' she replied.

Michael rolled his eyes then leaned over her shoulder and scooped a gloop of cake mix from the spoon. Before Mum had time to react, he smeared it on her nose and laughed.

Mum laughed back. 'Get off,' she giggled, and playfully pushed him on the shoulder. It was so soppy and gross, even worse than with Simon. As Mum pushed him, Michael lost his footing and stumbled back into the kitchen counter. He knocked into it and rattled one of the mugs on the top. It teetered on the edge of the counter. *Here we go again*, I thought. But then I looked a little closer. And that's when everything happened in slow motion.

'No!' I cried, dashing forward. But it was too late. The mug toppled over the edge and crashed onto the floor.

SMASH!

The sound echoed round and round the room. Nobody said anything. I looked down. The *World's Best Dad* mug lay shattered into tiny pieces. Ruined. I felt a lump form in my throat. My stomach felt sick. Dad's mug. It was the only thing I'd ever bought him that I had left. One of the only things to remind me of him.

Mum clapped her hand to her mouth, but Michael just shrugged his shoulders. 'It's no big deal,' he said. 'I'll buy you another one.'

152

'You can't buy another one,' Simon said, levelling his gaze at Michael. 'Some things are priceless.'

I didn't know what I wanted to do first – run at Michael and punch him a million times in the stomach or run away, hoping never to see his smug, annoying, horrible face again. Instead, I bent down to pick up the remaining fragments. I had to try and save it. Blu-Tack it together somehow.

Mum gasped and bent down to stop me. 'Don't,' she said softly. 'You'll cut yourself.' She looked at me and put her hand to my cheek. 'I'm so sorry, love,' she whispered. I didn't say anything.

Then Mum looked at Simon for what felt like for ever. 'He's not to do anything,' she told him eventually, 'but he can help you with your marking, or whatever it is you do,' and she gestured to Simon's clipboard. She gave me a small smile, and I could tell she felt bad about what had just happened. 'I'll be there in a bit,' she said. 'Go.'

Simon and I walked to the village green in silence. Even though Mum had finally said I could get involved, I couldn't stop thinking about the mug. I saw it fall from the counter top over and over again. It was all Michael's fault. All of it. 'He didn't even care!' I shouted out loud.

Simon looked down at me in surprise, but he must have

153

guessed what I'd meant because he said, 'I'm so sorry, Luke. It obviously meant a lot to you.'

I nodded. 'I got it him for Father's Day.' I'd saved up my pocket money for ages to buy it. Dad had been so pleased. I could see the smile on his face now as he opened it. He'd gone straight to the fridge and poured a protein shake into it.

'Are you up to this?' Simon asked as we turned the corner to the village green. I gulped and nodded my head. Michael wasn't going to ruin *this* for me as well.

Villagers and tourists crowded onto the green. There must have been five or six hundred of them. I'd never seen so many people gathered in one place in Port Bren. They squeezed into any space they could find that hadn't been taken over by the builders' materials. Despite the squash, everyone was in fantastically good spirits, determined not to be defeated by the sabotaging of the green.

I was angry at Michael for smashing Dad's mug and not seeming to care, but I thought if anything would wipe the smug look off his face, this would.

Then Mum and Michael walked onto the green. Michael looked back and clicked the alarm on his sports car then slung his arm round Mum. *Urgh*.

Simon glanced at his clipboard. 'So, it's Barry next, please,' he said. Grandad Barry, in vest and shorts, held up his boxing gloves. Simon shook his head. 'Uh, no. The Other Barry.'

'Right.' Grandad Barry frowned and stood back in line.

No one moved. 'He's gone,' Michael said. I could see he was trying not to laugh, but nobody else noticed.

'What d'you mean?' I asked, glowering at him.

'The Other Barry. He took the money and scarpered.'

Grandad Barry snorted in disgust. 'Typical,' he muttered. Gwyn sobbed into her hanky at the news that another one of the old guard had upped and left, and she leaned her head on Grandad Barry's shoulder, so he calmed down a bit.

'He had such lovely hair,' Gwyn wept. Grandad Barry frowned again.

'What can we do now?' I asked. 'Simon?'

Simon nodded towards the whiteboard. 'Well, you've registered a certain number of attempts,' he replied. 'If you can think of another, you can replace it – I've no problem with that.'

The whole village fell silent as we started to think of another attempt. Grandad Barry scratched his head. His special-occasion toupee (April Fool's Day) moved slightly out of place. He fixed it quickly and checked that no one else had seen. Grandad Barry was always doing that, yet was completely oblivious to the fact that the whole village *knew* he wore a toupee, special occasion or otherwise.

Simon cleared his throat and looked over at Mum. 'Mary?'

Mum raised her eyebrows at him. 'What can I do?' she asked.

Silence. The wind whistled through the green. Nobody said anything. What exactly *could* Mum do? She didn't work, because she said looking after me and Grandad Barry was a full-time job, and I'd never really seen her do anything apart from that, other than bake cakes. She couldn't play tennis, or twirl a baton, or generally do anything that would break a record.

'Lots of things, I'm sure,' Simon said, filling the silence.

Glyn stepped forward and gave her a wink. 'What about a kiss?' he suggested with a cheeky grin. 'The most kisses from the most men in a minute? You could do that.'

Mum shook her head. 'I don't think anyone would want to—' She stopped mid-sentence as a group of elderly men elbowed each other to get to her. They formed a line in front of her and started puckering up.

'I'd say any man would love to kiss you,' Simon laughed. Mum looked directly at him and smiled. He blushed immediately, realizing what he'd just said. 'For the record, I mean,' he added hastily. 'To, uh, to save the village.'

I figured it was as good an idea for a record attempt as any. Even if it was a little gross. 'Please, Mum,' I said.

Mum crossed her arms. 'No,' she stated firmly. 'I'm not getting involved.'

'Why not?' I asked. 'It's just one record.'

'I said no.'

I couldn't believe it. She'd only just said that I could help, so why did she have to be so stubborn? Didn't she want to save the graveyard? I kicked my BMX in frustration. I knew I shouldn't have, but Mum made me so angry sometimes.

Mum looked apologetically at Michael for the way I had treated his gift, which was rich considering how he'd just broken Dad's mug. She grabbed me by the arm. 'If you can't behave,' she said through gritted teeth. 'Home. Now.'

I tried to resist – I didn't want to stop the attempts, not when we'd come this far. 'Why are you being like this?' I asked. 'Dad would want you to—'

Mum stopped in her tracks. The villagers looked on in silence. I knew I'd crossed the line, smashed mug or no smashed mug. 'Dad would want me to what?' Mum asked in a soft voice, a steely glint in her eye. I didn't say anything and just hung my head. 'Become as obsessed with records as he was?' she continued. She started to blink hard, like I did when I didn't want Tim to see me cry. 'It was his whole

157

life, Luke,' Mum said. 'And now it's taking over yours. This has to stop.'

'But it's to save him!' I cried.

'No buts!' she replied. She lowered her voice and bit her lip. 'I buy you the books and the DVDs because I know you love it. It makes you feel close to your dad, I get that. And I'm sorry about his mug, but this is far enough.'

Mum pointed a finger at Simon as the whole crowd looked on. 'Don't get my son involved again, do you hear?' she snapped. Mum dragged me off by the arm, which meant end of conversation, and end of records for me. Almost as soon as I had begun, my involvement with the village's attempts was over.

Chapter Thirteen

That evening, just before bed, I sat at the kitchen table in silence and thought about what had happened on the green. Dad had loved records, so I loved them. Everything about them. It killed me not to be able to take part, but I knew better than to cross Mum.

So I did the next best thing I could do and flicked through my record book of 1981. Mum took another concoction from the oven. Brown goo dripped from the edges of the cake.

Frome Tourist wandered into the kitchen and helped himself to a bag of crisps. 'Need to get my strength up,' he spluttered, his mouth full of ready salted. 'Busy day sightseeing tomorrow. First stop, the Blarney Stone.'

I looked up from my record book. 'That's Ireland,' I told him.

'Right,' Frome Tourist replied.

Nobody said anything for a moment.

'We're not in Ireland,' I told him.

Frome Tourist stopped munching. 'What?'

I frowned at him. 'This is Port Bren, in Jersey. You came because you saw the records on the telly.'

'Records?' Frome Tourist asked. He scratched his bushy black beard, clearly confused.

I sighed. I couldn't be bothered to explain, and talking about records when I couldn't take part just made me sad.

Simon appeared in the doorway. 'I'm off to the village hall for Jill's attempt,' he said. 'You can come with me if you want. Most wine glasses smashed during an opera song.'

Frome Tourist shook his head in disbelief. 'I did wonder what everyone was up to,' he said. 'Just thought you were all a bit mad, that's all.'

Simon smiled and looked at Mum. 'They are,' he said, but I could tell he meant it kindly. Mum didn't reply.

As the door slammed, I absent-mindedly flicked through the record book, bored, frustrated and sad. Mum waited until the coast was clear and then sat down next to me at the kitchen table. She pushed a plate, with a slice of the brown cake on it, towards me. 'Full of vitamins and nutrients, that,' she said, and motioned to my height chart on the kitchen wall. 'It'll make you grow big and strong. Just like your dad.'

I didn't want to eat it, but I was already in enough trouble. I took a bite, and even though it was possibly the most disgusting cake Mum had ever made, I pretended to like it. It was Marmite delight, but without the delight part.

Mum stroked my hair. 'You understand, don't you, love?' she said. 'No more records. Not after everything that's happened.' She smiled down at my annual. 'The books are OK, though.' She kissed me on the forehead and returned to the kitchen worktop to clean the cake bowls.

I looked down at my book and flicked through the pages again. Something caught my eye and I leaned in for a closer look. I opened my mouth in shock. Smack bang in the middle of the page I'd turned to was Lloyd, his white ear hair tied into bunches. He looked almost as happy then as he had when driving his flash silver sports car on Tuesday. He held a certificate, and was shaking hands with a world-record adjudicator. Next to him was the caption: *Lloyd Blenkinsop, record holder for longest ear hair.*

'I don't believe it!' I cried. 'He's already broken a record!'

'What's that, love?' Mum looked up from the kitchen worktop.

I hesitated. I couldn't tell her, not when she'd just given me the speech forbidding me from taking part. But I had to let Simon know we'd already had a successful world-record attempt before all this started. Lloyd had taken the money and left the village before he knew of our plans, but he could still help save Port Bren. I knew I had no other choice

– I'd have to lie to Mum. But it would be a White Lie, so it was sort of A-OK.

I jumped up and shoved on my trainers. 'I've left my bike outside,' I said, trying to think of a plausible excuse for going out. 'I'll just put it in the shed.' Mum nodded and carried on with the washing up.

I got to the village hall in record quick time. Not an actual record, but pretty fast. I got there so fast that I could see Frome Tourist heading inside the village hall, whilst Simon stopped to check his clipboard. I dumped my BMX and ran towards him.

The sound of laughter drifted from the back of the village hall and Simon went to investigate. I followed at a discreet distance.

It was Michael, laughing with a woman. She wasn't from the village, so she must have been a tourist. She was very pretty, with long blonde hair, and she wore a pink top which showed off a small purple ring through her belly button. Michael laughed again and then leaned in towards the woman. They started to kiss. My stomach flipped over in disgust. *What about Mum?*

I was about to run forward and pull him off her, whoever she was, when Simon cleared his throat. 'What do you think you're doing?' he asked, trying to keep his voice steady.

Michael jumped away from the woman, panic flashing across his face. Then he realized it was just Simon. 'Has it been so long you've forgotten?' he laughed.

Simon blushed and pulled at his tie. 'Now, look here,' he said. 'What about Luke? They're a family. You have . . . a responsibility.'

Michael rolled his eyes. 'That family of hers are lucky to have me.'

Lucky? I couldn't believe it! Michael had signed the land over to the waste plant, he'd sabotaged our attempts to save the village, he'd snogged another woman and smashed Dad's mug, all in the space of a week. I could feel my cheeks grow red as I thought about how much I hated him. I was about to say, 'Enough is enough,' and, 'Here I am, what about me, Michael?' when Simon whispered, 'I know exactly what you're up to.'

So I held back a moment.

'I saw the deeds,' Simon continued.

Michael's smile disappeared. He gestured for the tourist to leave and she slunk off, away from the hall.

Michael grabbed Simon by the collar and slammed him against the wall. 'You shut your mouth,' he hissed into his face. Simon struggled to free himself, but Michael's grip was strong. Just like Tim's was with me.

'*You* sold the land, not your father,' Simon squeaked out

163

in between breaths. 'I'll tell the whole village what you're up to.'

Michael laughed. 'Oh yeah?' He put his face right up to Simon's, so their noses were almost touching. 'Prove it. Who are they going to believe? Me, an upstanding citizen of the village? Or you, who they've known for two minutes?'

Simon twisted his neck to speak. 'I *can* prove it,' he replied shakily. 'I've got the paperwork with your signature on it.'

Michael's eyes flashed with rage and his face contorted into a grotesque smile. 'Then I'll have you done for theft,' he sneered.

'Why are you so keen to destroy this village?' Simon managed to stutter. 'It's wonderful. I've lived in the same flat in London for the past ten years and I barely even know my neighbours. Admittedly, I'm always flying off around the world, but would a cup of coffee and a chat with Clive next door really be too much to ask? Even if Clive does keep ferrets. In his wardrobe.'

Michael gave Simon a strange look at this unexpected outburst. 'God, you're a freak,' he muttered under his breath.

'There's more to life than money, you know,' Simon continued through gritted teeth. 'What about community spirit? History?'

Michael looked away. 'You sound just like my father,' he eventually replied. His voice was soft, but shaking. 'He was always banging on about the importance of village life. He put it before everything and anyone else. Before me.' Michael blinked hard as his gaze drifted off into the distance. 'Dad was always too busy planning town meetings or organizing village fairs to worry about me. So I'm glad the old fool died and I sold the land. The plant will tear up this village and that's exactly what he wouldn't have wanted. Serves him right. It serves them all right.'

I caught a glint of sorrow in Michael's eye. It passed almost instantaneously, and a look of anger returned. 'And I get my money, so it's all win-win,' Michael hissed.

From inside the village hall Grandad Barry's voice called out, 'Simon? We're ready to start.'

Michael stared at Simon for a long moment and then released him. Simon massaged his neck. 'Village life is history,' Michael hissed in his ear.

Grandad Barry broke the silence. 'Come and do your job, man,' he yelled. 'It's why you're here.'

Michael smirked again, his anger now gone. 'Run along, Simon,' he laughed. 'You have a *responsibility*.'

Simon smoothed down his suit jacket and joined Grandad Barry at the front of the hall. Grandad Barry motioned to the stream of cars driving into the village over the creaking bridge. 'They're flooding in, Simon,' he said, unable to contain his excitement. 'Flooding in like a flood. It's doing wonders for our confidence, let me tell you.' Grandad Barry patted Simon on the back. 'We'll not be defeated, son.'

Michael followed Grandad Barry's gaze and glowered at the sheer volume of spectators. Hundreds more people were pouring into the village, in cars, on bikes and on foot. And there was another cartwheeler too. I smiled – clearly that wasn't part of Michael's master plan.

I snuck over to the window of the village hall and stood on my tiptoes. Inside, Simon stood in front of the villagers wearing a pair of grey felt earmuffs as Jill, whom Grandad Barry always called 'buxom' – which I figured had something to do with her large teeth and an even larger set of lungs – sang by a table of wine glasses. Jill opened her mouth and hit a long high note. It reverberated around the hall.

SMASH! The windows shattered under the strain. Glass flew everywhere. I ducked as shards of it rained down on me. What was it with everyone smashing everything today?

Villagers ducked for safety. Gwyn stumbled as she bent down, but Grandad Barry caught her. He gently helped her to her feet and Gwyn planted a kiss on his cheek in gratitude. Grandad Barry blushed at the unexpected result.

I looked down at my arm and gave a little cry. It had been cut by glass and a small trickle of blood dripped from the wound. My head felt dizzy, but I took a deep breath and willed myself not to faint.

Before I knew it, I sensed someone towering over me.

It was Simon. I expected him to ask what I was doing there, but he didn't say anything. Instead he took his hanky from his pocket and pressed it to the wound on my arm. 'That's it,' Simon said in a serious tone. 'It's going to have to come off, I'm afraid. I'll get a saw.'

I panicked. 'What?'

'Joke!' Simon smiled gently. 'You'll live. Though if your mum finds out you're here, it'll be a different story.'

I shrugged. 'So? You need me.'

'No I don't,' Simon replied. 'I'm fine.'

Well, that was just charming. There I was, glass stuck in my arm, trying to help with the records, even though I'd disobeyed Mum by doing so, and there was Simon saying that he didn't even need me. Simon must have thought the exact same thing, because he hastily added, 'No, no, I meant, I didn't mean . . .'

Except he couldn't quite get the words out. 'I've never had help before,' Simon said eventually. 'I've always managed on my own.' He took a deep breath and then asked something he'd obviously wanted to know ever since

167

he'd arrived in Port Bren. 'What happened to your dad?'

Well, that was a bit out of the blue. *What was Simon talking about Dad for? He didn't even know him.* But I still wanted to help with the records, and I figured that Simon could let me help without telling Mum, so I started to talk. 'Dad always said if you want something badly enough, you'll get it.' I squeezed the cut on my arm.

Simon laughed and I looked up at him. 'Are you saying my dad was wrong?'

'No,' Simon replied. 'It's . . . things aren't always that simple. Just because you want something doesn't mean it's going to happen.'

It sounded simple enough to me. 'Why not?' I asked.

'Because that's not the way the world works,' Simon replied. 'I want to do a million things: climb Mount Everest, sing with an African tribe. I want to – to fall in love.' He stopped and gave a big sigh. 'It doesn't matter,' he added hastily, 'because I'm never going to do it.'

I stared back at him. Why was Simon telling me this? And how wrong could one man be? 'Of course you're not,' I replied. 'You can't even tell Mum you fancy her. But I'm not you.' I looked down at the ground. 'I just want to help with the records,' I said. 'It's not fair.'

Simon smiled at me. 'It's not fair,' he said, 'until March. That's when spring starts.'

Just like Dad used to say.

Except Dad wasn't here. He was never going to be here, never ever, ever again. And no amount of wishing and hoping he'd come back would change that.

But Simon *was* here, and he was smiling at me, and something in his smile made me feel like it *would* be OK.

So I opened up and told him everything. It all came tumbling out – everything I'd been thinking about and worrying about for ever. 'I'm clever for my age,' I said. 'At maths and figures and stuff, and I remember things.'

'I had noticed,' Simon replied, and nodded at me to carry on.

'I'm only ten and I start secondary school this year,' I told him, speaking quickly to get it all out before I started to cry. 'I'll be the youngest. A whole year younger. And the smallest. And I don't have a dad. So I just wanted to break records. I don't want to be known as the small, brainy kid with the dead dad. At school, in September, I want to be known as the one who broke all the records.'

I wiped my nose on my sleeve. It was the first time I'd spoken about this to anyone, but telling Simon felt like the right thing to do. At any rate, I felt a lot better talking to Simon about it than I ever would have done to Michael. Good thing too, because when Michael wasn't smashing the most precious thing I had, he

169

was off snogging some other woman who wasn't Mum.

'He wanted to be the world's strongest man,' I continued. 'Dad. He was always jogging and training and trying to break world records. His heart just stopped one day. He bought me a new record book and an ice cream, and then his heart just stopped.' That was a year ago, but it felt like just one day. Mere minutes. It was all still as clear as anything in my head. The ice cream had a flake in it. 'He really was the world's best dad.'

Simon didn't say anything for the longest time, but just squeezed my shoulder. 'To thine own self be true,' he said eventually.

I wasn't sure what Simon was banging on about. What did that have to do with anything? It didn't even make sense. He might as well be spouting Russian, or Shakespeare, or something.

'It means just be yourself,' Simon explained. 'That's all you can be.'

'What do you know?' I replied. 'You said a boy at your school used to tease you.'

Simon drew himself up to his full height. 'Well, there you go,' he countered. 'Voice of experience. I didn't turn out too badly, did I?' He gave a small smile. 'Considering you wanted Vinnie Denton, not me.'

I shrugged. It was all very well Simon saying this, but

none of it mattered, not really. 'Whatever,' I said, and wiped my nose on my sleeve again. 'You're only here for the records and then you'll be off.' Simon would leave me, just like my dad had done. Well, not die, obviously, but he'd leave Port Bren and I'd never see him again.

'You know, Michael's a real idiot,' I said. 'I mean, I hate him and he sold the land and smashed my dad's mug, and all that. But at least he goes for what he wants.'

Simon started to protest, though deep down he must have known I was right. He looked off into the distance. 'I don't normally stay with the locals,' he sighed after a moment.

'I know,' I interrupted, picking up my BMX. 'It might be frowned upon.'

Simon smiled. 'I wasn't going to say that,' he said. 'I was going to say how much I've enjoyed it. Being part of the village. Part of a family.'

I didn't feel like talking any more. It was cold, it was late, my arm hurt – and pretty soon Mum would figure out I'd been far too long putting my bike in the shed, so I decided to go home.

I dashed across Dead Glyn's farmland, wondering how to sneak back into the house without Mum catching me. I'd had to tell the odd White Lie in my life, living as I did with Mum's baking, but if she found out I'd directly disobeyed her to watch the record attempts, I didn't know what she would do.

I pulled up at our front door to see Mum deep in conversation with Michael. I didn't want to face him, and explaining to Mum why I'd disobeyed her again was a whole other headache, so I snuck off to the vegetable patch and hid there until the coast was clear.

After a while I heard Simon's voice. 'Everything all right?' he asked Mum, and I sneaked back and saw that Michael had gone.

Mum scowled at him. 'I said no to Luke helping you,' she snapped.

'I didn't realize he was there,' Simon replied.

Mum looked him over to see if he was lying. She spotted blood on his hand and softened. 'Are you hurt?' she asked gently.

Simon glanced at his hand. He shrugged. 'I hadn't even noticed. I'm fine.'

Mum pressed a tissue to his hand. 'Well, aren't you the macho man?'

Simon laughed and Mum joined in with him. He cleared his throat and seized the opportunity. He knew I'd been right about just going for what you want. 'Uh, if you ever wanted to go out with me . . .' he stuttered. 'I mean, just for a coffee, or something.' Simon blushed. Then he took Mum's hand and kissed it gently. 'I like you, Mary,' he said. 'A lot.'

Mum smiled at him and clasped his hand. 'You are quite possibly the strangest, most awkward, most sensible man I've ever met,' she whispered. 'But I like you too.'

Simon pulled at his tie. 'Thanks,' he replied. 'I think.' And then he frowned. 'Look, I know it's Michael that you're with—'

Mum interrupted him with a sigh. 'Don't talk to me about Michael,' she said. 'He's in the doghouse.'

'I saw,' Simon replied. 'I take it he told you, then.'

Mum nodded. 'I can't believe he'd do that.'

'I know,' Simon said. 'She can't have been long out of her teens.'

Mum gave him a funny look. 'What?'

'The girl,' Simon replied. He caught Mum's *Explain yourself immediately* look. She clearly hadn't been talking about Michael snogging the tourist. Simon panicked. 'Oh, God,' he stuttered. 'Were you talking about Michael selling the land?'

'*WHAT?*' Mum cried. Now she looked utterly confused. Simon panicked a little more. She clearly hadn't been talking about Michael selling the land, either.

Mum released Simon's hand. I knew he was in for it. 'That's what you were arguing about,' Simon added meekly. 'Wasn't it?'

Mum opened her mouth in shock. 'We were arguing because Michael bought Luke another present,' she said. 'And I told him he was spoiling him.'

'Oh,' Simon replied quietly.

'Yes. *Oh.*' Mum didn't look impressed. 'Michael kissed another woman?'

Simon nodded.

'When? And why didn't you tell me?'

Simon shrugged. 'Just now, but – it wasn't my place—' he started.

Mum's eyes flashed with anger. 'But you knew about him selling the land?' she thundered on. 'Why didn't you tell me about that?'

'I tried to,' Simon protested.

'Tried to?' Mum yelled, getting angrier by the second. 'Is that all you've got?'

Simon didn't reply. You could have heard a pin drop.

'Forget it,' Mum fumed, and barged past him. 'I'm going to give Michael what for.'

'Don't go!' Simon called after her, but Mum stormed off down the lane.

'You go,' she yelled back, not turning round. 'Home. Your real home. Just go.'

I was about to jump up and run after Mum, glad that the truth about Michael had all come out when Simon's phone rang. 'Ha!' Simon cried, taking the mobile from his pocket. 'I've got a signal! Finally!' He snapped open the phone and ran about the garden, trying to get the best reception he could, so I ducked down again. I wasn't in the mood to carry on our 'talk' from the village hall.

The caller was Max, booming down the phone just as loudly as he always did. 'Good news, Simon!' he roared at him down the line. 'I'm no longer thinking of sacking you. In fact, I'm promoting you. That job in Australia? It's yours.'

Simon was confused. 'What? I don't understand.'

'You'll be on the DVD, Simon. *You!*' Max waited for a response. Simon rubbed his temples as he took it all in.

'I thought you wanted this?' Max said.

'I did,' Simon replied. 'I mean, uh, I do. Of course I do. What about Vinnie?'

Max sighed. 'Too cocky for his own good. It's you, Simon. I knew it would be.'

Simon straightened his tie and wiped away a tear. 'Uh, th-thank you, sir,' he stuttered.

'You fly tomorrow,' Max continued. 'If you leave now, you can catch—'

'*Now?*' Simon interrupted, panic flashing across his face. 'Port Bren has just a few more hours.'

'Don't worry about that,' Max replied matter-of-factly. 'I'm sending another adjudicator.'

175

'But there's no time,' Simon protested.

'He's already on his way.'

There was no point arguing with Max. Simon looked around the garden, but he didn't spot me. '*Go home*,' Simon whispered to himself, echoing Mum's words. '*Your real home*.' He let out a long sigh. 'Of course,' he said into the phone. 'I'll collect my car and leave straight away.'

Simon hung up, placed the phone back in his pocket and coughed to cover his tears.

I'd had enough. Everyone was arguing with each other. Simon was giving up on us and leaving. *What was the point?* I climbed back on my BMX and pedalled off, desperate to clear my head.

On the way I spotted Michael over at the bridge. He was in the middle of an argument with Mr Pringle-Bliss. 'There's no more room!' Michael yelled so loudly I could hear everything. He gestured to all the tourists on the other side of the bridge, beeping their horns in sheer delight at having finally arrived in Port Bren.

Mr Pringle-Bliss was having none of it. 'This is *exactly* what we wanted,' he insisted. 'Outsiders coming into the village, spending money in our shops. And with all this support, there's no way we'll fail. The waste plant will never be built.'

Michael didn't reply. Instead he barged past Mr Pringle-Bliss and stormed off into the night.

I pedalled over to the graveyard and sat on my bike by Dad's grave. My conversation with Simon had brought up so many feelings: about how Dad had died, about starting secondary school this year. And there was what Simon had said about just being yourself. 'Just being yourself is all very well and good,' I muttered under my breath, 'if you actually *like* being yourself.'

So much had happened in the last few days, and my head hurt from thinking about it all. I got off my bike and lay on the ground next to Dad's gravestone. The grass felt cool on my cheek and I closed my eyes to try to stop the world spinning.

I didn't even realize I'd been asleep when a loud noise, like an engine revving, boomed across the graveyard. I leaped up and squinted to see what was happening. It was Michael, sitting in a fork-lift truck by the bridge. He watched the stream of cars drive over the ancient, rickety bridge into Port Bren and grinned a maniacal grin. It stretched all the way from one ear to the other, his eyes shining brightly. He gripped the steering wheel of the fork-lift truck, pulled a lever and drove forward to meet the tourists head on. *Now what was he playing at?*

Michael drove the truck repeatedly back and forth over the bridge. *'Flooding in like a flood?'* he shouted, the mad grin still plastered on his stupid face. 'I don't think so!'

Spectators and tourists all tooted their car horns in frustration as Michael's crazy driving blocked their entry into Port Bren, the village they'd seen so much of on the news. But worse than that, thanks to Michael's efforts with the fork-lift truck, big cracks began to appear on the surface of the ancient bridge. It shook more than ever. Pleased with his handiwork, Michael reversed off the bridge and made his way back to his mansion. 'Serves you all right!' he shouted to anyone who would listen.

I had to tell someone. The whole village had to know what Michael was up to, even if Simon was abandoning us. I wiped my face with my palms, turned my BMX round and pedalled off as fast as I could.

The village was eerily quiet. I checked my watch, and my eyes almost bulged out my head when I saw it was well past my bedtime, even for school holidays. Mum was going to go mental!

As I raced over Dead Glyn's farmland towards home I heard a car in the distance. It was Simon driving towards the bridge, on his way to the ferry. Sir Walter was strapped, in his glass case, into the passenger seat beside him. The sounds of an African tribe burst from the car's CD player, their voices exuberant and powerful. 'Simon!' I shouted, but the music was so loud he didn't hear. It was too loud to even hear the old, cracked bridge groan under the weight of his car. The bridge swayed unsteadily over the quarry, as the tail-lights of Simon's car receded as he drove away from Port Bren.

Then I saw Mum in the tractor, racing after Simon as fast as she could. And suddenly it all made sense. All those times Mum had pretended to roll her eyes at Simon but then laughed her head off at something he'd said made me realize that, for the first time since Dad had died, Mum had been happy. Truly happy. And that's all she'd wanted. She *had* to stop him from leaving.

I pedalled after her as quickly as I could, but the tractor was going too fast. 'Mum!' I yelled. I tried to warn her but she couldn't hear. *What was it with everyone going deaf all of a sudden?*

The bridge creaked and groaned as Mum drove over it, unable to cope with the strain any longer. An almighty *CRASH!* rang out through the village and the bridge finally gave way. The crash was so loud, everyone in Port Bren was sure to have heard it, whether they were deaf or not.

A gaping hole appeared in the middle of the bridge as it tore in two, and a *CLANG* rang out when the two halves dropped to the bottom of the quarry. It all happened so quickly, Mum didn't have time to hit the brakes. The gaping hole where the bridge had been swallowed up the tractor – and Mum with it. She hit her head on the steering wheel as the tractor fell forward, through the gap and tumbled down, down into the darkness.

Sunday
Chapter Fourteen

Brakes screeched to a halt and tourists jumped out of their cars to see what had happened. The bridge hung in two parts, an empty black hole in the middle.

'Mum? Mum?' I shouted. I looked down into the quarry, but it was too dark to see anything. I got off my BMX and hopped from one foot to the other, desperate to find out if Mum was OK.

And then I heard her voice. 'Luke?' Mum sounded faint and distant. 'Thank God. Where've you been?'

'Dad's grave. I fell asleep. Are you OK?'

'I'm fine,' Mum replied. 'But you need to get help!'

I was torn. I didn't want to leave her, but I knew she couldn't get out of the quarry on her own.

I felt a hand on my shoulder and turned to see Walking-Stick Glyn looking down on me, still clutching Miribel's lead. 'Go phone an ambulance,' he said softly. 'I'll stay with your mum.'

I cycled home and burst into our kitchen, grabbed the

phone and punched in 999. 'Grandad?' I shouted while I waited for someone to answer. 'Tourist Guy?' I glanced around the kitchen and spotted the empty space on the sideboard where Sir Walter's case and Simon's briefcase had been. Before I could call out again, a voice answered the phone. 'That sandwich filled a hole,' it said. And then, 'Emergency, how can I help you?'

'Ambulance!' I shouted into the phone. 'Please. Come quickly.'

After I'd given them all the details, I put down the phone and took a few breaths to gather myself. Then I spotted something on the table. I leaned in for a closer look. Dad's mug stood in the centre of the table, intact. It had a large crack down the middle, so that it read WOR D'S BE T DAD but it looked almost as good as new. Before I could even begin to wonder where it had come from, I spotted two pieces of paper lying next to it. One had *To thine own self be true* written on it; on the other, under a yellow stain that looked suspiciously like gecko's wee, I saw *DEEDS TO THE LAND*. I recognized the green curling leaves of the official stamp, and flew out of the door.

I pedalled back to the quarry, dumped my BMX and kneeled down at the edge of the fallen bridge. 'The ambulance is on its way!' I shouted down to Mum.

'You're a good lad, Luke,' Mum replied, taking deep breaths. Her ragged breathing carried all the way to the top of the quarry, and I could tell she was trying not to panic.

'It *was* Michael, all along,' I shouted. I held out the wee-stained paperwork to her, to confirm what Simon had accidentally admitted, but it was so dark I didn't know if she could see.

Glyn looked down on me in surprise, but before I could explain, the blare of sirens rang out. Tourists parted as an ambulance screeched to a halt at the other end of the bridge and a paramedic jumped out. He looked at the fallen bridge, then down into the quarry. 'Blimey,' he said to himself. He scratched his head and called to his partner, 'We're going to need a bigger van.'

His partner looked confused – Port Bren didn't have bigger vans. The paramedic sighed. 'I meant, the other way in – via Marvel Barton – is too narrow. We're going to need something else to get across this bridge.' He leant across the driver's seat and picked up his radio.

While he called for a fire engine, his partner got out of the ambulance and shone a torch down into the quarry. And what a sight it was. Mum was on the ground, dust and dirt on all her clothes. She was holding her ankle in pain. The tractor was upturned in the distance. The two halves of the bridge had completely smashed on impact and were lying in pieces all over the quarry floor.

I cupped my hand to my mouth and shouted down, 'Mum! Are you sure you're all right?'

Mum nodded weakly. 'I'm fine,' she replied, but I could tell by her voice that she wasn't. 'I just want to get out.'

The paramedic smiled kindly at me. 'She's lucky. The tractor broke her fall. Just a sprained ankle, I suspect,' he said. 'She'll be fine as soon as I can put some ice on it.' Then he reached into his pocket and pulled out a digital camera. 'Though while I'm here . . .' He shrugged. He snapped away on his camera at me, Mum and all the tourists.

I didn't know what else to do, and I didn't want to leave Mum, so I sat down by the edge of the quarry and waited. That's when everything that had happened in the last few days finally hit me. I'd tried so hard not to cry in front of anybody, but I couldn't fight it any more. I sobbed and sobbed and sobbed like there was no tomorrow. 'I'm not crying,' I shouted down to Mum, tears streaming down my face. 'I've just drunk too much water.' My eyes felt all red and sore and my lungs puffed like bellows as I fought for breath in between my sobs. I felt as if I'd never, ever stop.

Chapter Fifteen

I yawned sleepily. Everything was so hectic at the bridge; there was zero chance of sleeping. I'd never seen so much action in Port Bren. Grandad Barry had arrived to offer his support, Miribel was mooing like a fog horn and all the tourists and spectators kept beeping their horns. Daffydd and the male choir had popped up out of nowhere, their red cardigans all tatty and three days' worth of stubble on their chins, but they kept singing nonetheless. Some people in this village were still determined not to be defeated.

The fire engine had arrived and all the fire crew were standing around, debating with the paramedics about the best way down into the quarry.

'What you need is a system of ropes,' one paramedic was saying.

The chief fireman shook his head. 'Only a crazy person would hoist themselves down there,' he said. 'We'll use the crane.' He waved to Mum. 'We'll soon get you out, love,' he called.

Mum gave him a weary smile and then shouted up to

me. 'You heard, Luke! Don't worry about me.' And then she said something I never thought I'd *ever* hear her say. *Ever*. 'You've got to carry on with the records.'

It took a moment for me to register what she'd just said. 'What? You hate records!' I yelled back. I knew just being stuck in a quarry wouldn't stop her.

Mum smiled. 'But *you* don't, and that's the main thing. I've had time to think down here, and we have to carry on trying to save the village. We've only got a few hours left. Glyn told me. We're so close.'

Wow. This was unexpected. Mum was actively *encouraging* me to get involved with the records. But the more I thought about it, the more I realized there was no point. 'Simon's gone and you're trapped,' I called down. 'Michael's won,' I muttered under my breath.

Grandad Barry squeezed my shoulder. 'No,' he said firmly. 'I won't let you give up.' He nodded towards the ever-singing, ever-present male choir. 'After this lot, we only need one more pass!' Grandad Barry had a sudden thought. 'Hang on a bean,' he boomed. 'Jill didn't complete her record attempt! All the glasses smashed, but so did everything else. There was no way we could count them all. For the love of *Bergerac*! We need another attempt! To break our fiftieth. We need a new record!' Grandad Barry smiled at me. 'Why don't you have another go?'

I thought back to the list of records for me to hold before I was older. The International Space Station was a long way off, and I'd already failed in the cup stacking. 'I could squirt milk from my eye?' I said, slightly unsure what Mum would make of this, regardless of her sudden change of heart.

Then another thought popped into my head. *Mum!* 'Mum could help!' I yelled. 'Well, not technically, she's stuck under the bridge.'

'How then?' Grandad Barry asked, and he scratched his head in bemusement. His toupee shifted slightly, but I politely pretended not to see.

'Well,' I continued, my mind going like the clappers. 'Mum can help with, um, baking! She's always baking cakes, right?'

'If you can call them that,' Grandad Barry replied with a frown.

'I heard that,' Mum grumbled from down in the quarry.

I leaped up in excitement. 'No, *we* can bake. The most cakes – wait!' I remembered all the cakes I'd stacked against the kitchen wall, ready for the council's consumption.

'A tower of cake!' I cried. 'The world's tallest cake!' I couldn't believe I hadn't thought of it before.

Mum grinned. 'Capital idea, Luke,' she called.

Grandad Barry reached into his pocket and passed me a

set of keys to his shop. 'You get going. I'll stay here with your mum.'

I leaned over the side of the bridge to look at Mum one last time. 'Are you sure?' I asked.

'You were right, love,' she called back. 'Your dad would want you to do it. I'm sorry I've been like this. I was—' She paused. This was hard for her to say. Especially in front of an army of tourists she'd never seen before in her life. 'I was scared,' she said. 'But I can't stop you from living your life, and I shouldn't stop you.'

And then I finally understood why Mum had banned me from taking part in the village's record attempts. Dad had died of a heart attack after trying to be the world's strongest man for so many years. The doctors at the hospital had said that Dad had had an irregular heart beat and the amount of vigorous training he'd undertaken had finally taken its toll. Mum was scared that, somehow, I would go too far, like Dad had done. She couldn't bear to think that she might lose me too.

'I'll never do anything dangerous, Mum,' I shouted down into the quarry. 'Not like Dad.'

Mum wiped a tear from her eye. 'I know, love,' she replied. 'But life is for living. So, go on! No time to lose!'

I hated to leave her down there again, in pain, but she'd finally given her blessing for me to get involved in the record attempts. I was about to jump back on my bike, but stopped myself in time. Just six days ago, I'd have said it was the best present since sliced bread – if you happen to think sliced bread makes a good present. But now I knew exactly what Michael had been up to, and how he'd caused the bridge to break and Mum to fall in the quarry, I didn't want anything more to do with him or his gifts. Even if it meant I'd never see Sir Winston again, it was a price I was willing to pay. I kicked the BMX for good measure and Mum didn't even say anything. Largely because she wasn't looking.

I knew what had to be done. I wasn't allowed to do it last time, but now there was no stopping me. I ran from house to house like a madman, spreading news of the last-minute, last-ditch record attempt. Villagers were bleary-eyed and sleepy as they opened their doors, but they soon leaped into action. What with everything that had happened last night I'd forgotten to tell Simon about Lloyd's former record success, and even though Simon had gone, there still wouldn't be time to track Lloyd down to verify it anyway. We *had* to break one more record to meet the required fifty that would make us famous and stop the waste plant. We *had* to save the village. And my dad.

I was about to burst through our front door when Frome Tourist opened it. As well as one sock with stripes and one sock with frogs on it, he wore a pink dressing gown fastened by a zip, clearly having made himself at home – it was Mum's.

'A tower of cake?' Frome Tourist mused after I'd told him of the plan.

'Uh-huh.' I nodded. 'But we've only got four hours till time's up.'

Frome Tourist grinned. 'Well then,' he replied, 'what are we waiting for?'

Crammed like sardines into Grandad Barry's village shop, me, Frome Tourist, Gwyn and as many villagers as could fit inside swiped the shelves clear of cake. 'Grab as many cakes as you can,' Frome Tourist shouted to everyone. 'And don't spare the Battenberg!'

The village green was still the hub of the operation, even though it was swamped by building materials. I found the whiteboard and scrubbed it. I wiped out the attempt that said *OPERA WINE GLASSES, JILL*, and replaced it with, *TOWER OF CAKE, VILLAGE*.

Beaming torches around the green to see what they were doing, villagers tore open boxes and, in a line, passed the cakes to me. In one of the few spaces free of building materials, I formed a base for the tower.

Having got wind of this new venture, the TV news crew buzzed around me. 'Think this'll work?' the reporter asked me, shoving a microphone into my face.

I shrugged. 'Why wouldn't it? We've got to try.'

The TV reporter smirked. 'Just thought you were trying to have your cake and eat it, that's all,' he replied.

I didn't stop what I was doing, but I allowed myself to laugh. 'That's terrible,' I groaned.

In homes around Port Bren, villagers baked like they'd never baked before. Because most of them hadn't. Eggs were dropped onto the floor, but scooped into bowls anyway, wedding rings were accidentally kneaded into dough, smoke alarms beeped throughout the village as cakes burned in ovens. Turns out Mum wasn't the only one who couldn't bake.

As dawn broke and the sun rose over Port Bren, Jimmy arrived at the front of the production line and tugged on my sleeve. 'They're getting your mum out,' he panted.

I forced my way to the front of the quarry, just as the chief fireman signalled for his crew to release the cherry-picker crane from the top of the fire engine. The fireman opened the cab and climbed inside. He pulled a lever, and with a click and a whirr the crane slowly extended out across the quarry.

At that precise moment a car screeched into view. All the spectators and tourists jostled out of the way as someone pushed to the front of the crowd. I squinted to see what the fuss was about. And then I saw him.

It was Simon.

He elbowed his way to the front of the bridge and looked down into the quarry. 'Mary!' he shouted, cupping his hand to his mouth. Mum shielded her eyes from the sun and gasped when she saw Simon. He had returned!

'You came back!' I cried, not caring that I was stating the obvious.

'She was on the news,' Simon shouted to everyone. 'About the fallen bridge. I got as far as Weymouth and I had to come back.'

The TV reporter nodded to his film crew. 'We've hit the big time, people,' he beamed.

Down in the quarry Mum was fanning herself to keep cool. 'I'm so thirsty,' she called weakly.

Simon bit his lip as he saw Mum wilting in the heat, looking like she might faint at any moment. 'She needs water!' he cried.

From somewhere at the back of the crowd, a plastic water bottle flew through the air. It smacked Mum squarely on the forehead. The force knocked her over and she keeled onto the ground.

'For goodness' sake!' Simon cried, looking wildly round the bridge. 'Why is she still down there?'

The cherry picker creaked unhealthily as it extended over the quarry. Inch. By. Inch.

It was too much for Simon. He tugged off his suit jacket, tied it round his waist and shuffled to the edge of the quarry. 'Keep it together, man,' he muttered to himself. 'You can do this. Just don't look down.' He looked down, and almost cried in fear. 'What did I just say?' Simon berated himself.

The fireman glanced over at him. 'What do you think you're doing?'

Simon shook his head. 'I'm – I'm not sure,' he said. 'No, wait, I am sure. I'm going to rescue her.' He pointed at the crane. 'But if you think I'm going in that, you've got another think coming. I had enough of that in Norway, thank you very much. Panic attack halfway up the world's tallest Christmas tree.'

The fireman shook his head. 'I can't let you, man,' he replied. 'Health and safety, for one.' Simon inched forward regardless.

From the village side of the bridge, I saw Michael appear to witness the commotion. Tim, Owen and Izzy lagged behind.

Mum pointed a finger at Michael when she saw him. 'Don't you come anywhere near me,' she yelled. 'You've caused enough damage.'

'He told you, then,' Michael replied, casting a steely glare in Simon's direction. 'I did you a favour by signing those deeds, Mary.' He looked around at the villagers. 'I did you all a favour. You can finally get out of this backward backwater.'

Everyone murmured to each other. *What did he mean?* Only Glyn, Simon, Mum and I knew all about Michael's sabotage, but there was no time to explain.

'How dare you make that decision for me?' Mum cried. 'For anyone?'

Michael stepped forward to the edge of the quarry. 'I – I still love you,' he said, not totally convinced, or indeed convincing.

'No you don't,' Mum cried. 'You never did. You just wanted me as some sort of trophy. Someone else to buy for, to stop you getting bored.' She took a deep breath. 'And if I'm honest, I only dated you to get over Scott,' she said. 'I wasn't ready to deal with his death, but now I am. And you are the last person I want to help me.'

Frome Tourist nudged Glyn in delight. 'Should have bought popcorn,' he said, grinning.

Michael produced a small box from his pocket. He opened it and a dazzling diamond ring shone in the sun. Villagers shielded their eyes from the brightness of the gemstone. 'Will you marry me?' Michael shouted down into the quarry.

'No way!' I shouted before I knew what I was doing.

Hadn't he just heard what Mum had said? 'Don't you dare!'

Mum laughed. 'I wasn't going to say yes,' she called up.

'Good,' I replied. 'Because Simon would make a better husband than him.' I glared at Michael and thought back to the patched-up mug on the kitchen table. 'And a better dad.' Mum didn't say anything, but even from the edge of the quarry, I could see her turn red. It might have been sunburn, though.

Michael put the ring back in his pocket. He looked defeated, but he didn't give up. 'I'll save you,' he shouted down to Mum, moving towards the edge of the quarry. 'You'll see.'

The fireman sighed from the other side of the bridge. 'Just what we need,' he said to himself. 'Another have-a-go hero.'

'No!' Simon yelled, 'I was going to . . .' But his cries were lost in the chatter of the tourists.

The fireman pulled a lever and the cherry-picker crane started to move a little faster. It jerked forward and gave another unhealthy groan. And then it just stopped altogether. The fireman scratched his head and looked at the levers. He tried harder. The crane jerked again, let out a mechanical shriek and then gave up, once and for all.

Frome Tourist nudged Glyn once more. 'This is better than *EastEnders*,' he said with glee.

Michael shouted down into the quarry. 'I'm coming for you,' he said to Mum. He took a deep breath, but didn't move forward.

'Well, go on, then,' Frome Tourist said after a while. A flicker of panic crossed Michael's face.

'She probably wants saving *today*,' Glyn chipped in.

Michael lifted one foot up and over the edge of the quarry. Slowly, so slowly – even slower than the cherry-picker crane, and that wasn't even moving – he started to lower himself down the rock face. The village waited with bated breath.

Then all of a sudden Michael stood bolt upright. 'Nope,' he said, 'can't do it.'

'You afraid of heights, or something?' Glyn asked.

Michael was careful to avoid Tim's gaze. 'Me?' he spluttered, trying hard not to sound panicked. 'Afraid? Don't be ridiculous.'

'Then go and rescue the woman you love.'

For once, Michael didn't know what to say or do. He wanted to rescue Mum, if only to prove how macho he was, but the quarry just seemed so deep.

From the other side of the bridge, Simon lowered himself down the rock face. 'Well, stone me!' Frome Tourist cried, and pointed over at him. 'Simon's doing it.'

Sweating profusely, Simon inched himself down the quarry. His foot slipped and the crowd gasped as one as he stumbled. Simon shot out his hands to steady himself against the rock face.

Beside me on the village side of the bridge, Daffydd, still singing, started leaping about and pointing frantically. 'What are you doing, man?' Grandad Barry boomed, but Daffydd couldn't break from the tune. Instead he pointed to his tatty red cardigan and then mimed pulling on a rope, back and forth.

'Two words?' Grandad Barry cried, clearly confused. 'Sounds like . . . ?' Daffydd shook his head in frustration and then took off his cardigan. He pointed across the quarry at everybody. 'Have you gone mad?' Grandad Barry asked. 'Or are you just hot?'

I looked across at all the spectators on the other side of the fallen bridge, some of whom were wearing light sweaters and cardigans. And one American family who insisted on wearing plastic ponchos, despite the glorious sunshine. 'I think he wants everyone over there to take off their cardies,' I said slowly, trying to decipher Daffydd's gestures.

Daffydd gave me a thumbs-up. He made a pulling motion again.

'And tie them together?' I asked. 'Like a giant rope?'

Daffydd beamed and jumped up and down on the spot.

'Well, why didn't you just say so?' I laughed. I cupped my hands over my mouth and shouted to everyone over the

197

bridge. 'Take off anything with sleeves and tie them all together!' I yelled. 'Then chuck the rope to Simon.'

Everyone did it immediately, chattering excitedly as they whipped off their tops. They formed a line and passed each item forward, stringing them together.

'Just like scout camp, this,' I heard someone cry in delight. 'And I've got a woggle on me.'

One spectator made his way to the edge of the quarry and held the makeshift rope out to Simon.

Simon took it gratefully and tied it to his jacket sleeve. He tugged at it firmly to see if it would hold. It was surprisingly solid. The spectators took the end of the cardigan-chain and held it firmly like a giant tug-of-war.

Simon held onto the rope of cardigans as if his life depended on it. Which worked out well, considering it did. He lowered himself down the quarry, whilst everyone bore his weight. Tourists and villagers looked on with a mixture of awe and bemusement. Even the chief fireman was impressed. 'Easy does it!' he yelled, getting caught up in the moment. His crew looked up at him. 'Uh, I mean, stop!' he blustered. 'Health and safety!'

'Wait!' the paramedic cried, ducking into the ambulance. He emerged with an ice pack. 'Give her this!' He chucked it down to Simon, who shifted his hold on the rope of cardigans to catch it.

'Heave, ho, heave, ho,' Daffydd and the choir boomed, launching into a sea shanty as the spectators heaved on the rope. 'Haul and pull and hoist! Some have died, some—'

'Yes, we'll leave that there, thanks,' Simon shouted back, his face knotted in concentration. 'Right, God,' he said to himself in between breaths. 'We both know I'm not a religious man. But if you could just make sure that I live, I'd very much appreciate it—'

He slipped slightly, but managed to catch himself. Everyone gasped. 'Yes, thanks for that, God,' Simon said, looking up to the heavens. 'Good to have you on board.'

From the village side of the bridge, the TV reporter motioned to his camerawoman and smoothed his jacket. 'Amazing scenes unfolding here,' he said into the camera. 'Scenes of bravery – or stupidity, depending which way you look at it. But meanwhile the village has one last attempt up its sleeve. Port Bren has spoken, and that word is *cake*!'

Simon landed at the bottom of the quarry. He tugged off his jacket, regained his composure and ran over to Mum.

She hugged him gratefully. 'You did it,' she cried. 'I'm so proud.'

Simon strapped the ice pack to Mum's ankle and gently hoisted her up onto her feet. He slung an arm round her shoulders in support and together they limped to the other side of the quarry. 'I'm sorry I shouted at you,' Mum said softly. The last time she'd seen Simon, she'd told him to leave the village – to get out for good.

Simon beamed back at her. 'I've heard the world's loudest shout,' he said. 'Believe me, your yelling was nothing.' They both laughed as they started their ascent.

Climbing back out was just as tricky, and Simon had to keep shoving Mum's bum to push her up the other side. He didn't look like he minded too much, though.

We all peered over the edge as they slowly ascended. Simon was concentrating so hard on not falling, his tongue stuck out of the side of his mouth and, even from the top of the quarry, I could see the sweat on his forehead.

But Mum was clearly struggling. 'My ankle!' she cried out, leaning against the rock face for support. Seeing her visible pain, Simon didn't hesitate. He edged his way over to Mum, and threw her arms around his neck. Then, with all the grace of a hippo, and huffing and puffing like it was going out of fashion, Simon carried Mum out of the quarry, piggy-back style. He tottered unsteadily as he tried to keep his balance, Mum clinging on all the while.

After a moment, Simon reached into his pocket for his hanky and almost lost his footing. All the loose change from his pocket fell out as he leaned into the rock face to steady himself.

'About forty-nine pence, I reckon,' Frome Tourist shouted down as the coins landed at the bottom of the quarry.

'You all right there?' Mum asked as Simon battled on.

Simon closed his eyes and took a moment to catch his breath. 'Quite fine,' he managed to gasp. But he didn't look it. He braced himself and carried on scrambling up with Mum on his back. After what felt like for ever, their heads appeared at the top of the quarry.

Frome Tourist and Grandad Barry reached down to haul Simon and Mum up, and everyone on both sides of the bridge broke out in applause as they shakily set foot on solid ground. 'Good show!' Frome Tourist cried. 'Encore! Encore!'

Grandad Barry slapped Simon on the back in celebration, as Michael stormed off in a huff. He obviously couldn't believe that someone like Simon had succeeded where he was too afraid to try. Grandad Barry noticed him leave and pointed right at him. 'Never mind all those parachuting photos of yours, Michael,' he said, and slapped Simon on the back again. 'This is what a real hero looks like.'

Simon smiled. It turned out Michael wasn't such the action man after all – the pictures in his glass cabinet must have been fake. 'One word,' Simon grinned. 'Photoshop.'

Knowing it could be done without loss of life or limb and desperate to enter the village, tourists on the other side of the bridge followed Simon's lead, and one by one they scrambled down the quarry.

'You could always enter the village via Marvel Barton, you know,' the paramedic called out to them.

'Wouldn't be half as much fun then, would it?' one tourist cheerfully replied.

The fire crew raced to hold onto the rope of cardigans for added support as tourists climbed down the quarry and into the village. The chief fireman tried to protest from the broken crane, but nobody paid the slightest bit of attention to him. 'Stop!' he cried, but even his own crew ignored him.

Grandad Barry checked his watch. 'An hour to save Port Bren!' he shouted. 'To the tower!'

'What tower?' Simon asked. Jimmy, Grandad Barry, Glyn, Frome Tourist, Mum and I shook our heads. 'Long story,' we all replied in unison.

Simon looked down at Mum's strapped ankle, and then back to the other side of the bridge. 'My car's over there,' he said, nodding. Shifting Miribel's dog lead in his hand, Glyn reached into his pocket and threw Simon his car keys. 'Use mine, it'll be quicker.'

It was a Mini. With little choice, Simon helped Mum inside and climbed into the car. As did Grandad Barry, Gwyn, Frome Tourist and seven other villagers, just for the fun of it. It could have been a world record in itself.

Simon turned to grin at me. 'I've got a present for you,'

he said, and opened the top pocket of his shirt. He gently pulled out Sir Walter.

'What?' I shouted. *Sir Walter, my present?*

'He was so sad about leaving the village,' Simon explained, 'he went right off his food. I've a whole tub of crickets in my car, completely untouched. What do you say? Will you promise to look after him?'

I nodded and held out my hand. I scooped up Sir Walter into my palms and smiled in delight. 'It's the best gift ever,' I said.

Mum sighed, but I could tell she didn't really mind. 'You coming with us, love?' she said.

I saw how cramped the Mini was and shook my head. 'See you on the green,' I said.

Simon revved the engine and sped off into the village, quicker than I'd ever seen anyone drive in Port Bren. It was our special rule, see. What with all the tractors and cattle-herding going on, no one was allowed to drive above ten miles per hour.

Still, we had bigger fish to fry. I placed Sir Walter in the pocket of my T-shirt and together, Jimmy and I ran off towards the Tower of Cake.

We didn't go straight there, though, because just then, something happened. Something painful and scary and brilliant.

Chapter Sixteen

Tim stepped in front of Jimmy and me as we ran towards the village green, and stuck out his foot. I didn't see it and went flying. I landed awkwardly, feeling the skin come off my knees. I looked down and saw that they were both grazed. I felt my pocket to make sure that Sir Walter was OK, and a lump formed in my throat. 'Why are you doing this?' I asked softly.

Tim laughed cruelly. 'Because I can.'

Hot pricks of blinding pain appeared behind my eyes, but I knew I couldn't let myself cry. 'You're a bully,' I said. 'And Simon says that bullies are just cowards.'

Tim rolled his eyes. 'Don't give me that,' he said. 'Simon knew you were a loser, that's why he did one and left. Like a coward.'

I tried to muster as much confidence as I could. 'Takes a loser to know a loser,' I replied. I realized what I'd just said – that I'd made a hash of what I thought was a witty comeback. 'W-wait,' I stuttered. 'I meant you're a loser for calling me one, not that me or Simon are losers.'

'You're a bigger geek than I thought!' Tim smirked back at me. 'And I thought your mum and her cakes were weird. No wonder your Dad keeled over and died. She probably poisoned him with a cyanide crumble.' He leaned over and laughed right in my face.

That was it! I finally saw red. Enough was enough. Tim bullied me – fine. Tim made jokes about my dead dad and his uncle smashed my dead dad's mug – not fine, but I'd put up with it. But insulting my mum, who last night I thought I'd lost as well? So Not Fine. It was just about enough to send me over the edge.

'My mum's cakes are the most nutritious in Port Bren,' I said through gritted teeth.

Tim shrugged. 'So?'

It was now or never. 'So,' I began slowly, 'she may not be as rich as you, but she loves me, and she loves this village, and we'd never sell the land like your uncle did. And at least my mum wants me, which is more than could be said for your parents.' My voice grew stronger by the second. 'So you're the loser, Tim. You and your family.'

Tim was shocked. In all these years, I'd never spoken to him like that before. I could have sworn I saw tears in his eyes, but after a moment he got a hold of himself. He motioned for Owen to punch Jimmy in retaliation for my outburst, but Owen hesitated, and I could see that he didn't want to follow instructions this time. Tim gestured again. After a moment, and with what looked like regret etched onto his face, Owen punched Jimmy in the stomach. Jimmy doubled over in pain.

'Apologize and I'll let him go,' Tim said. I got to my feet slowly. 'I'm sorry,' I replied softly. I took a deep breath and gritted my teeth again. 'I'm sorry I didn't do this sooner.' Gently, ever so gently, I pulled Sir Walter from my T-shirt pocket.

'What are you doing?' Tim asked, and I could see the panic in his eyes.

'Got a little present for you,' I laughed, and I held Sir Walter in front of me, right up to Tim's nose. The colour drained from his face and he squirmed just as much as I remembered him squirming every other time he'd been near Sir Walter. That's what gave me the idea, see.

'Get off!' Tim cried, stumbling backwards as he tried to get away from me. I shook Sir Walter at him once more, and Tim cried out in a mixture of fear and disgust. 'Get away!' he cried in a high-pitched whine. 'I don't like it!'

He tried to run away, but tripped over his feet and fell flat on his back. Owen and Izzy couldn't help it – they burst out laughing.

I punched the air in delight for what felt like the millionth time that week, though this time I *really* meant it.

'*Yesssssss!*' I cried. I couldn't believe it. After years of being teased, taunted, punched and bullied by Tim, it felt so good to get my own back. 'Well done, Sir Walter,' I whispered to him, and placed him gently back in my top pocket. I could have stayed all day to gloat, but then I remembered the records. I reached down to help Jimmy to his feet. 'Let's go,' I said.

Jimmy kicked Owen in the shins for good measure and together we ran off to the green.

The Tower of Cake stood almost two metres tall. Jimmy and I rejoined the group, and the production line of villagers worked fervently, adding layer upon layer. Mr Pringle-Bliss and three council officials looked on. Simon walked around the cake, taking it all in. It looked amazing. Layers and layers of different desserts – sponge cakes, carrot cakes, Battenberg – were piled high in a circle that worked its way up to the heavens. It was like cake Jenga.

A villager held out a cake to Simon, but he hesitated. 'Is Vinnie here yet?' he asked me.

I didn't look up from the tower, just continued working. 'Vinnie who?' I replied. I didn't have time for this.

Simon smiled. *Vinnie who?* I'd just said. Only a few days ago, all I'd wanted was Vinnie. 'Obviously not,' Simon said. He grinned to the cake-holding villager. 'I'm sorry, I can't get involved. I'm adjudicating.' He turned to me again. 'Right?'

This time I gave him a long look. Part of me wanted to tell Simon no for walking out on the village. For walking out on Mum and me. He'd upped and left without even saying goodbye. Just like Dad had.

But – and it was a big but – Simon had come back. When he saw that Mum was in trouble, when he knew we needed help, he'd come back. And he'd come back with a vengeance, saving Mum when no one else would. 'About flaming time,' I replied.

Simon laughed. Mum shot me one of her *Mind your language* looks, but she couldn't quite hide a smile.

I stood on tiptoe to add to the tower, but I couldn't reach the top. It had grown too high for me. Mum took the cake and added more tiers herself. 'We're going to need a ladder,' she remarked. 'And honey.' She caught Simon giving her a curious look. 'Trust me,' she laughed.

'Right you are,' Glyn said, tugging Miribel by the lead. 'Shan't be long.'

More and more cakes were added to the production line from villagers who'd collected them at the fallen bridge. Hundreds of tourists unable to enter the village had tossed their cakes over the quarry, right into the arms of the waiting villagers, though some cakes had crumbled on impact.

Glyn returned to the production line on the village

green, juggling jars of honey and a wooden ladder. The ladder was barely taller than me, so not exactly what I'd had in mind. Izzy joined the line with the crumbling cakes as Glyn set up the ladder by the tower.

From out of nowhere the choir popped up and launched into the hearty chorus of a song all about some guy called Jacob climbing ladders. Spurred on by the music, I did just that. I climbed the ladder as far as I could go and added more tiers to the tower.

But the ladder still didn't take me high enough.

'What are we going to do?' I cried as I scooted back down. I could feel one of my panics coming on. The villagers looked up in dismay. No one knew what to do.

Simon locked eyes with me and cleared his throat. 'Bald Head,' he coughed into his hand discreetly.

Nobody said anything. Then Grandad Barry stepped out of the production line and shook his fist at Simon. 'How dare you!' he shouted.

Simon looked confused, but coughed into his hand again. 'Bald Head,' he repeated, a little louder this time.

Grandad Barry let out a big sigh and his shoulders slumped in frustration. He whipped off his special-occasion toupee (Ramadan) and revealed his natural, shiny bald head. His secret was finally out. 'How could you tell?' he asked softly.

Everyone stared at him in amusement. Mum and I rolled

our eyes, knowing this day had been a long time coming. Grandad Barry tucked his toupee in his pocket and avoided Gwyn's gaze.

'No, no, that's not it,' I said, my mind whirring. '*Bald Head . . .*'

Grandad Barry interrupted me, clearly annoyed. 'All right!' he shouted. 'So I'm bald! Get over it! The toupees were a terrible mistake.'

I ignored Grandad Barry's outburst and carried on with my thoughts. 'It's a town in Maine,' I said to myself. 'They built – oh, what was it?'

Inspiration struck. 'The world's tallest human pyramid!' I cried. 'By standing on each other's shoulders! That's it!'

Simon winked at me – I was spot on. I leaped into action, knowing exactly what needed to be done. Out of the corner of my eye, I saw Izzy stare at me with a funny look on her face. Almost like admiration.

I looked at the gaggle of villagers and spectators gathered on the green and pulled from the crowd a stocky, heavy-set man with broad shoulders. 'Do you think you could lift someone?' I asked.

The man flexed his muscles and all the ladies in the crowd gasped.

'Been training for the Olympics since I was seven,' he replied. 'I'm going for weightlifting gold.'

I smiled, impressed. 'Well, then,' I said, 'you can be the base.' I looked around the crowd again, taking charge. 'And we need someone tall.'

Standing – literally – head and shoulders above everyone else was a two-metre-tall man. 'That'll be you, then,' I smiled. He may not have been Robert Wadlow, but he would do.

The heavy-set man braced himself and grabbed the tall man's foot. 'My name's Steve,' the heavy-set man said in a growly voice.

'Paul,' the tall man replied.

Which was all very well, but I didn't think they had any time for niceties. Steve, the heavy-set man, hoisted Tall Paul up onto his shoulders. Steve swayed slightly at the heavy load, but then steadied himself. The villagers passed cakes to Tall Paul and he added them to the tower.

Mum smeared honey round the edges of a crumbling cake, like Dad used to when he filled in the cracks in Grandad Barry's walls for him. Though, just for the record, Dad never used honey in Grandad Barry's walls. It looked awful but it kept the cake together. 'You don't have to eat it,' Mum smiled as she caught Gwyn staring at her.

'Thank God for that,' Gwyn replied.

The Tower of Cake stood almost four metres high, seven cakes wide. *The Leaning Tower of Port Bren.* Simon checked his watch. 'Forty minutes to go,' he informed us.

211

'The current world's tallest cake is six point seven metres,' I said, and looked up at the tower. 'We need to get higher.'

Mum tried to rally the troops. 'Come on, team!' she cried. 'We can do it!' Mum passed the cakes onwards with gusto. All the fun she was having was clearly making up for falling in the quarry. She took her eyes off the cakes she was passing and levelled her gaze at Simon. 'You know, open collar really suits you,' she said.

Simon felt for his tie, and then remembered that he'd discarded it at the bridge. 'Thanks,' he replied. 'Oh, I see – no buttons.'

'No,' Mum explained, 'I meant, it makes you look more handsome. More relaxed—' And then she screamed. Loudly. She looked down at her hands and saw that she was holding a cake in the shape of A GIRAFFE! Mum dropped the cake, and clutched at her throat. 'Suspiciously. Long. Necks,' she stuttered, breathing deeply. She stumbled backwards in shock and knocked into the tower. Several tiers collapsed.

'I'm sorry,' someone shouted from the back of the production line. 'It was all they had left in the supermarket. But it is fair trade, if that helps?'

Simon and I both rushed over to Mum. Simon gently helped her to her feet and guided her back to the line. 'It's

OK,' he soothed. 'I'm right here. You've conquered the buttons. You can do this.'

Mum nodded and continued to breathe deeply. She took a moment to regain her composure.

I bent down and picked up the giraffe cake. I thrust it into Simon's hands and ran back to the base of the tower.

Simon smiled as he held the giraffe cake out to Mum. She hesitated, but then took it from him. She held the cake gingerly and passed it along to Tall Paul, who added it to the tower.

I looked up at the Tower of Cake. 'How tall is it now?' I asked, concerned we were running out of time.

Grandad Barry held a finger up to the wind. 'About fifteen metres, I reckon.'

I rolled my eyes. *Not strictly true, Grandad*, I thought, but I didn't say anything. I could see that he was trying, even though he was still upset about being outed as a baldie.

Simon felt in his trouser pocket and whipped out a tape measure. He winked at me. 'I always carry a spare,' he said. He walked forward to measure the cake, his tape measure held aloft.

CLICK! A handcuff clamped around Simon's wrist and a policeman frowned at him. 'I don't think so, boyo,' he said.

Everyone gasped in shock. 'Simon David?' the policeman continued. 'I'm arresting you on suspicion of speeding.'

Chapter Seventeen

Mum hobbled forward. 'Speeding? What do you mean?'

'You do not have to say anything—' the policeman recited.

Simon interrupted. 'Rats! You mean on the motorway from Weymouth? I had to get to Mary.'

The policeman faltered. 'Motorway?' he asked. 'I was talking about speeding through Port Bren, but if you've offended twice . . .'

Simon forced a smile. 'No, uh, just kidding about that,' he blustered.

Michael stepped out of the line of villagers. 'Well, this doesn't bode very well,' he smirked.

Urgh. I couldn't stand the sight of him. Trust him to try and ruin everything. He was determined, I'd give him that.

'Haven't you done enough?' Mum cried.

Michael held up his hands in protest. 'I'm just a law-abiding citizen, doing my duty, reporting crime,' he said with a sneer.

'I'll sort this out,' Simon said to the villagers and squared up to Michael. 'Did you see me speeding?' he asked him in an even tone.

'Of course I did,' Michael replied. 'In Glyn's Mini, from the bridge to the green. Just now. We have clear laws in Port Bren.'

Simon looked him straight in the eye. 'Prove it,' he said.

Michael's smile faded. *Oh, how the tables had turned!* 'What?'

Simon took a deep breath and spoke slowly, trying to keep his voice steady. 'Port Bren has many wonderful things,' he insisted. 'A village shop that always gives you service with a smile.'

Jane, the cashier in Grandad Barry's shop, glowed with pride. Nobody had ever said a nicer thing to her, even after she'd survived being held up at gunpoint by a gunless Gareth.

'An elderly man who wears fantastically bright lime-green swimming trunks.'

Gareth blushed with everyone looking at him. He pulled down the top of his trousers to reveal a patch of his thigh, and the crowd wolf-whistled as he showed off his swimming trunks once more.

'A family who have made me more welcome than I ever thought possible.'

Grandad Barry gave my shoulder a squeeze as we both beamed up at Simon.

'A wonderful, beautiful woman I've fallen head over heels in love with – zipped-up blouses and all.'

Mum couldn't hide her delight. She pushed him playfully as if she was dead embarrassed, but I could tell she was chuffed.

'And a very strange tourist from southwest England who can never wear socks of the same pattern.'

Frome Tourist didn't notice that the eyes of all the villagers, spectators and tourists were fixed firmly on his feet. 'Who's that, then?' he asked, confused.

'But what this village *doesn't* have,' Simon said calmly as he squared up to Michael, 'is speed cameras. Right? So technically, it's your word against mine.'

Michael couldn't believe it. 'You're not getting away with this,' he spluttered. 'The whole village saw you speeding.'

Simon looked around to the villagers before him and implored them, 'Did you?'

Nobody spoke.

Then I stepped forward. 'I didn't see anything,' I said firmly.

Mum smiled and joined in. 'Nor me,' she said, and winked down at me. White Lie or no White Lie, it was for the best.

Michael rolled his eyes. 'Oh, come on.'

Simon gestured to the individual villagers. 'Did you see anything?' he asked, gaining enthusiasm and courage as he spoke. 'What about you? Seen any speeding recently? You?'

'Nothing,' they all cried.

'Nope.'

'Not a thing!'

'I have!' a voice from the crowd piped up. Glyn leaned on his walking stick, deep in thought. 'About one hundred miles per hour, I reckon.'

Simon was incredulous. 'What?'

Then Glyn scratched his head in confusion. 'Oh – oh – wait a second,' he said. 'Nope, it wasn't Simon. I remember now. It was the Brazilian Grand Prix. On the telly.'

Simon waved his handcuffed wrist in the air. 'I know this puts you in an awkward position,' he said to the policeman, 'but do you mind? If there's no proof, you can't arrest me, and we've got a record to break.' He smiled. 'Of the non-criminal kind, of course.'

Michael gestured for the policeman to stand firm, but there was nothing he could do. The policeman shrugged and brushed Simon's shirt sleeve. 'Sorry about that,' he apologized. 'As you were.'

The crowd cheered as the policeman released Simon and all the villagers returned to stacking the tower with cake.

Simon checked his watch as he rubbed his wrist. 'You've

got thirty minutes,' he said to the crowd. He stepped forward to measure the tower again, but someone beat him to it.

A man peered out from behind the cake. 'You're just a few metres short,' he boomed, clutching a tape measure.

Simon was shocked. 'Max! *You're* the other adjudicator?' It was Simon's boss.

Max's tanned face wrinkled as he winked at Simon in a fatherly fashion. 'I was already on the ferry when I called you last night,' he roared. 'Couldn't let you have all the fun, could I—?'

But just then disaster struck! 'I can't do any more!' Tall Paul shouted down. He grimaced as he realized he couldn't reach higher to add cakes to the tower. And we still had so much more cake to go. Everyone stopped as they tried to figure out what to do next.

Simon motioned to Tall Paul. 'The human pyramid,' he said. 'Someone else needs to go up there.'

Mum shielded her eyes and looked at the top of the tower. 'What?' she exclaimed. 'No. It's too high.'

'I'll go!' I shouted. 'We need to break the record.'

Mum shook her head. 'If you fall, you'll break your neck.'

'But, Mum,' I pleaded. 'I have to!' I was desperate. We couldn't have come this far, only to fall at the final hurdle.

'No buts!' Mum replied. 'That's what your father said

and he died because he couldn't say no. He always had to push that little bit harder, train that little bit longer. I'm saying it now. No.' She fixed me with one of her *End of discussion* looks and that was that.

The villagers all hung back in hesitation. They gazed up at Tall Paul, and at the sheer height of the makeshift human ladder. They all wanted to save the village, but nobody was quite willing to climb so high to do it.

'I would go,' Grandad Barry stuttered, clutching his chains, 'but better not risk it. What would the village do without a mayor?'

'Twenty minutes,' Simon piped up.

'Come on!' I cried. I tried to appeal to the village. 'Someone! Please! It's for the village. Our homes. My dad.'

Nobody was quite willing to meet my eye.

Michael laughed as villagers turned to each other and shrugged their shoulders. And then I locked eyes with Simon. I could see him think about what needed to be done. Think long and hard. Longer and harder than if he were to take an advanced mental maths test, and the ones Mrs Wilson gave were pretty hard sometimes.

'Please!' I cried in despair.

Simon stirred into action. He stepped forward to Tall Paul and took a deep breath. 'Lift me up,' he said in as calm a voice as he could muster.

Mum opened her mouth in surprise. 'Not you as well!'

Michael looked at Simon as if he were mad. 'Haven't you forgotten something?' he asked. 'You're the adjudicator. You can't get involved.'

Glyn glimpsed at his watch. 'Fifteen minutes to go!' he cried.

Simon looked at Mum, and then at me. 'Fine,' he said defiantly. 'I quit.'

Mum, Michael, Max and I looked at Simon in shock. 'What?' we all said in unison.

'Max, I'm sorry,' Simon replied, conviction in his voice.

'But the job?' Max protested. 'The promotion?'

'I have to do this,' Simon stated calmly. He handed his clipboard and stopwatch over to Max, but he clung onto them a fraction longer than necessary. He expelled a decisive puff of air and finally let go.

Simon placed his foot on Steve's knee, ready to go. He gingerly clambered up the Olympic weightlifter, pausing to inhale deeply. Simon opened his eyes and realized that he'd paused right in front of Tall Paul's crotch. 'Sorry about that,' he muttered apologetically.

The crowd gasped as Tall Paul swayed slightly. But Simon ploughed on, climbing up Tall Paul's towering frame. He stepped onto the man's shoulders and tried to balance himself.

With precision finer than a Swiss watch, the male choir launched heartily into another song, crooning about being raised up and standing on mountains.

Simon secured more cakes on top of the tower, though he had to reach higher to keep building. I could see him trying to stand on tiptoe, but he still had a couple of centimetres to go until he reached the top. It looked like Simon couldn't get there.

'Reach up!' Mum shouted to him. 'Reach up!'

'I'm trying!' Simon shouted back down. 'I can't get any higher.'

The village was distraught. We weren't going to make it. We were going to fail!

I turned to Mum. 'Please,' I begged, not knowing what else to do. 'We've come this far.' And then I remembered what Mum had said down in the quarry. 'Life is for living, you said,' I cried. 'I've got to do this!'

'But it's too dangerous,' Mum blurted out. She had tears in her eyes.

Grandad Barry stepped forward and solemnly took off his gold chains. He then turned and clasped hands with Gwyn, positioning himself at the base of the tower. He encouraged the other villagers and tourists to do the same, and they all lined up at the bottom of the tower in support, their arms clutching each other tightly. 'It's a

221

safety net,' Grandad Barry told Mum. 'In case he falls.' He winked at me. 'Which he won't, will you, lad?'

I shook my head.

Mum thought it over for a moment. She glanced at her watch. After the longest time she gave her answer. 'Be careful,' she said to me, ever so softly.

I didn't have time to punch the air in delight and yell, *Yesssssssss!* even though that was what I wanted to do. I took Sir Walter out of my pocket and gave him to Jimmy to look after. Then I took a deep breath and put my left foot on Steve's knee.

Using all the strength I could muster, I held onto Steve's head for balance and hoisted myself up. Tall Paul reached down to grab my arm, and I shakily put my right foot the other side of Steve's head. I think I might have stood on his ear because he suddenly yelped in pain. My left foot somehow found Steve's other shoulder and I levelled up to Tall Paul's waist. He yanked me by the arm and I dug into his hip bone as a foothold. The movement made Tall Paul jerk, and he groaned in agony. Down on the ground I heard the crowd gasp as we all swayed – it looked like Tall Paul was going to fall.

I quickly shoved my right foot into the crook of his elbow and clambered up to his shoulders. Then Simon reached down to steady me. Tall Paul stopped swaying and seemed to find his balance. The crowd let out a sigh of relief as I hoisted myself up Simon's torso and placed my feet on his shoulders.

Simon's hands clasped around my ankles. 'I've got you, son,' he said. I slowly straightened all the way up and the crowd whistled and cheered. I'd done it!

I'd never been this high up in all my life, but I knew I couldn't panic. It was scary, being so high, at the top of a shaky, makeshift human ladder with only Grandad Barry and the other villagers beneath me for protection, but I had to stay calm for the village. For Dad.

I took long, deep breaths and allowed myself to look down as I caught all the cakes that the villagers and tourists hurled up to me. After a moment or two I found my bearings and I was able to catch more cakes. Fruit cake, arctic roll, sponge fingers – I added them all to the tower. It was perfect – we were almost there. I just needed to reach a bit higher and add a few more cakes . . .

But I couldn't do it. I had stretched up as far as I could. My ribs ached from stretching so much, and I heard a couple of bones crack in my shoulders.

We were still several centimetres from beating the record.

I cursed my height. *Why did I have to be so small?* If only I'd practised my secret reaching exercises more, I could have been taller. I could have reached as high as the tower

223

required me to, and added as many cakes as we needed.

That was it! *The exercises*. I looked down and saw the faces of the crowd below. They looked so small from up above. But I could see Tim's face clearly, a big stupid smirk on his big stupid face. I thought back to when I'd failed my cup-stacking attempt, just a few days earlier. Simon had said I could give it another go, but I hadn't wanted to in front of everyone, especially Tim.

Now I knew there was no other choice.

I took a deep breath. I didn't care what Tim – or anyone – thought. I knew what I had to do. I stood on the balls of my feet. To stop myself from swaying, I focused on a point far off in the distance. I took deep breaths and extended my chest through my side ribs, just like the yoga book I'd borrowed from the library told me to. Just like I'd practised.

The villagers gasped as I perfected my graceful, ballet-like move. 'Where did that come from?' Grandad Barry shouted up at me.

'My secret reaching exercises!' I shouted back down. 'To help me get taller.'

Grandad Barry smiled. 'Not so secret now, are they?'

I reached up as high as I could and added more cakes to the top of the tower.

The sound of the choir swelled, and Daffydd urged them to sing with gusto as I secured the last of the cakes.

'Nine minutes to go!' Glyn shouted.

Max bent down to the bottom of the tower and passed the tape measure up to Simon. He caught it and threaded it to me. I measured the very tip of the tower. 'Six metres, sixty centimetres,' I declared.

Mum threw more cakes up to Simon and me. 'Just a few more centimetres to go,' she cried. Simon caught the cakes, trying not to slip, and passed them up to me.

I finally positioned the last cake in place. It was a chocolate gateau that had melted slightly in the sun, so I made sure it was as secure as it could be and then held my sticky hands aloft. 'Done!' I cried triumphantly. I took the tape measure again. 'Six metres seventy one centimetres!' We'd done it!

Max beamed up at me. 'Well, that's a new world record,' he confirmed.

'*Awooga!*' someone at the back of the crowd shouted.

I punched the air in delight. 'Our fiftieth record!' I cried. 'We did it!'

Everyone cheered wildly – we had succeeded. *WE HAD SUCCEEDED!* Our homes would be saved, our community spared.

Villagers, tourists and spectators all went crazy. Crazier than they'd ever gone before, even for Port Bren. Grandad Barry jangled his ceremonial chains victoriously. One man

225

tried to start a conga line, but everyone was too busy hugging each other to notice so it was just him dancing on his own. Even Miribel mooed. She was probably just hungry, but we all took it as a moo of triumph.

Simon held onto my ankles as Tall Paul grabbed my waist and lifted me into the air. Using the tower as a buffer, he shakily placed me on Steve's shoulders and I jumped down to the ground in delight. Simon's descent wasn't quite so smooth. He managed to fall against the tower and kicked several cakes in the air on the way. Nobody cared, though. Villagers danced under the tower as carrot cake and bread and butter pudding rained down on them.

As Simon hit the ground with a thud, everyone rushed forward to slap us on the back in praise. Cheryl, the baker, got out her triangle, Roy Fort, the butcher, got out his tin trumpet, and his son blew a party whistle in celebration – never let it be said that Port Bren didn't know how to push the boat out. Even if it was with 'Jingle Bells'.

With our feet firmly on the ground, I ran over to Simon and hugged him. 'That was awesome,' I said, a lump forming in my throat.

'Piece of cake,' Simon replied, ruffling my hair. I grinned, and didn't think now was the time to mention how terrible his jokes were.

Tall Paul and Olympic weightlifter Steve scooped Simon

and me up once more and carried us around the green on their shoulders as if we'd just scored the winning goal in the cup final. I felt on top of the world.

Mr Pringle-Bliss jumped in the air with joy. 'You saved Port Bren!' he yelled. He glanced at his watch. 'And with four minutes to spare!'

The council officials all nodded in confirmation – fifty world records had been broken, Port Bren was now on the map, so the village had indeed been saved.

Mr Pringle-Bliss turned to Michael, sheer triumph on his face. 'The waste plant will *not* be going ahead.'

Michael laughed at him. Quietly at first, but then his eyes twinkled with glee and a deep laugh rose from the pit of his belly. It boomed all around the village green. Everyone looked at him curiously. After a moment Michael caught his breath and looked Mr Pringle-Bliss squarely in the eye. 'That's not strictly true now, is it?' he said in a low voice. 'The village hasn't been spared at all.'

Chapter Eighteen

A hush descended over Port Bren as the crowd quietened to hear Michael out, and Steve and Tall Paul lowered Simon and me to the ground.

Michael looked at his audience. 'It was agreed the waste plant wouldn't be built if you broke fifty records by eight a.m.,' he said.

'Can't you count?' I said. 'We did.'

Michael smirked back at me. 'No,' he replied slowly, as if he didn't realize just how clever for my age I was. 'The last record *didn't* count.'

The villagers all scoffed. 'Ignore him,' Mum said. 'He's talking rubbish.'

Michael's top lip curled into a snarl. 'If the record adjudicator gets involved,' he said calmly, 'the record attempt is disqualified. Blame your "boyfriend".'

'I quit, you snake!' Simon replied, holding his hands up in protest. 'You saw me. There was another adjudicator.'

Mum looked at Simon in horror. 'The giraffe cake,' she whispered. 'You passed it to me. When I stumbled.'

It took a moment for everyone to remember. I'd handed the giraffe cake to Simon and he'd passed it to Mum before Tall Paul had added it to the tower. 'I – I didn't mean . . .' Simon stuttered, panic creeping into his voice. 'Oh, God.'

'You broke the rules, Simon,' Michael said cruelly. 'And if anyone knows that rules are rules, it's you.' The villagers turned to Simon in shock.

I rushed forward and stood by his side. 'It's not his fault,' I cried. 'It was mine. I passed the cake to him.' I felt terrible. I couldn't believe it. I had been the one to fail. Me. After all our efforts, after all that I knew about world records it had been me who had let everyone down.

I turned to the village with tears in my eyes. 'We could try again,' I said, pleading to anyone who would listen. 'We'll start a new tower.' I knew it was no good, but we had to do something. We couldn't let Michael win.

Michael tapped his watch. 'In two minutes?' he taunted. 'I don't think so.'

Simon shook his head in despair. 'I should have realized,' he whispered. 'It's my fault.'

I was devastated; the village defeated.

Michael turned to Mr Pringle-Bliss and the council officials. 'Preparations for your inevitable failure have already been made,' he jeered, barely containing his excitement at our misery.

In the distance a loud crash rang out across the village.

I ran to the edge of the green and followed the sound of the noise. It had come from the graveyard. I strained to see and could just about make out a bulldozer driving over the land. With a flick of a lever the bulldozer's demolition ball swung again and crashed into the side of a gravestone.

I cried out in anguish. '*No!*' I couldn't see from this far away, but there was every chance the gravestone had been Dad's.

Michael placed a hand on my shoulder. 'You tried,' he said to me. 'That says a lot, son.'

Urgh. 'I'm not your son,' I replied. 'Get off me.' I twisted out of Michael's grasp. 'We were so close,' I said, not caring that tears had started to run down my cheeks.

Michael revelled in his victory, and in the sheer and utter dejection we villagers, tourists and spectators all felt. 'I wanted you to prove me wrong,' Michael said, smirking at all of us. 'You couldn't do it, though, could you?'

I felt the anger rise within me. He looked so smug.

Then, from nowhere, it came to me. The best idea that I had *ever* had.

I did it to wipe the smile off Michael's face. I did it because it felt like the best thing to do at the time. I did it because, suddenly, those thousands of people running through the streets of Spain didn't seem so crazy after all.

I ran over to the tower and scooped out a handful of cake from somewhere near the centre. It was one of Mum's leek surprises. I held it in my hands and then looked at Michael. 'Time for plan B!' I yelled and chucked the cake as hard as I could at Michael's face.

Time seemed to stand still. I watched as the leek surprise flew towards him. I could see Mum open her mouth in shock. Michael barely had time to react – he certainly didn't have time to duck.

THWACK! The cake hit him squarely on his forehead, crumbling on impact. Moist bits of leek slowly dripped down his face. Two or three seconds passed in which no one said anything.

Then everyone started to cheer.

Michael looked horrified. He wiped the cake off his face and threw the fragments back at me, but I was quick and ducked just in time.

I grabbed more cake from the tower. This time, I wasn't alone.

Simon scooped a handful of Victoria sponge from one of the tiers and threw it at Michael's head. He missed. 'Rats!' he cried.

THWACK! Michael threw the cake back at Simon and it hit him on the shoulder.

I picked up a slab of banana cake. 'This is for humiliating

my mum!' I shouted as I launched it at Michael.

Mum was already behind me. 'And that's for cheating on me – and the village, you prat!' She hurled a whole Battenberg at Michael and it hit him on the knee.

Grandad Barry stepped up and stared at all the cake. He picked up a chocolate log and went to throw it, but he couldn't help himself. He took a bite instead. 'I'm going to gorge myself,' he said greedily. The diet Mum had put him on had sent him a little crazy. 'I'm going to Cheddar Gorge myself!'

Mum shook her head firmly, so Grandad Barry threw the cake at Michael instead – his plastic-coconut-throwing skills finally paying off. He whipped out his toupee from his pocket and, for good measure, threw that at Michael too.

Taking their cue from me and my family, villagers and tourists grabbed armfuls and armfuls of cake and threw them all at Michael.

A fully-fledged cake fight descended on the green. Sponge, raisins, icing and honey were thrown around like there was no tomorrow. Everyone laughed and cheered, regardless of whether they actually hit Michael or not.

'The world's largest cake fight!' Gwyn giggled, hugging Grandad Barry in delight. 'Our fiftieth record!' She was so happy; she even took a bite of one of Mum's straw supremes with the smeared-on honey round the edges.

The dart players were putting their skills to good use and aimed sponge fingers at everyone in sight, throwing them like darts.

The German father of the very first tourist family that had come to Port Bren was snapping away on his camera, taking photos of his wife and daughters covered in marble cake.

THWACK! A lemon cheesecake flew through the air and smacked him on the arm. The German father dropped his camera in surprise. The flash went off and an unattractive picture of his left nostril was displayed on the screen.

Absurdly Old Dave shuffled around the green talking into his mobile. Or rather, shouting, such was the din. 'That's what I said!' he was yelling. 'Cake. No – cake. *CAKE!*'

THWACK! A walnut loaf smacked him right on the ear and the force knocked him backwards. He lost his footing and toppled into the Tower of Cake. He lay there, unable to get up, but everyone simply ignored him and carried on scooping gloop from the tower around him.

As the church clock chimed eight, villagers shrieked in delight, and chaos descended. Before long, it was impossible to tell who was who and everyone was completely covered.

'What's going on?' A voice suddenly rang out over the noise of the crowd. Mr Wilson stumbled onto the green, his legs sticking out of the bottom of his canoe, which was well and truly wedged round his waist. He wore a French beret on top of his head.

Mrs Wilson let out a shriek and ran forward. 'What happened to you?'

'Turns out I didn't have my reading glasses, after all,' he replied. 'Got a bit lost. Ended up in Calais. But then I got bored and ate a week's worth of Kendal Mint Cake in one day and the canoe capsized.'

Everyone burst out laughing. Mr Wilson looked hurt, but then noticed the events unfolding around him. He reached into his top pocket and grabbed the last of his Kendal Mint Cake stash. 'When in Rome!' he yelled, and launched the cake at Michael's head. It hit him right between the eyes.

'We're not in Rome,' Frome Tourist replied. 'It's Port Talbot.'

'Port Bren!' we all cried back, ignoring Absurdly Old Dave and picking up more cake from the tower.

In a matter of minutes Michael was submerged in a heap of Madeira cake and trifles, with the odd Jersey Royal potato and packet of couscous thrown in for good measure. 'HELP!' he cried.

The policeman took a message on his radio. 'Right-o,' he said back into the walkie-talkie. He moved to Michael, whose outstretched hand was just about visible from under the cake pile. The policeman pulled at it and helped him up.

'About time,' Michael huffed, getting to his feet. He tried to wipe the cake off his clothes, but the policeman kept hold of his hand.

'Mr Harding,' the policeman said firmly, 'I'm arresting you on suspicion of criminal damage.'

Michael stepped back in alarm. 'What?' he blustered. 'What's the meaning of this?'

The policeman gestured to the building materials swamping the green. 'You may have sold the farmland to the waste plant, but you don't own everything in Port Bren,' he said. 'Bringing all these diggers and breeze blocks onto public land constitutes criminal damage.'

The policeman motioned behind him to a builder who had taken off his hard hat and was right in the middle of throwing cake at anyone in sight. 'We've had a tip-off it was down to you,' the policeman explained. 'And we have witnesses placing you in a fork-lift truck just before the bridge collapsed. And don't get me started on smashing through gravestones.'

Michael started to protest, but then thought better of it. He'd finally been caught out. He ignored the cheers of the villagers as the policeman led him away in handcuffs.

But just as the policeman was putting Michael into the

police car, Glyn barged into him, his walking stick held high above his head. 'Run!' Glyn yelled, shuffling along as fast as he could. 'She's gone mad!'

A loud *moo* sounded from behind the tower, and villagers, tourists and spectators scattered as Miribel ran amok, cake smeared around her mouth.

'She's had too many E numbers!' Adam Leroux cried. 'What have you done?'

Miribel started thrashing about, trying to detach herself from the dog lead Glyn had by now let go of. Glyn blew his whistle in a last-ditch attempt to calm her down, but it was too late. Miribel scraped her front hoof repeatedly on the ground, and with a loud *MOOOOOO* of anguish chased after Glyn, following him all round the green.

'You wanted the bull-running!' Adam shouted, not even bothering to hide a smile.

The cow raced after Glyn, heading towards the police car, but at the last minute Miribel stopped dead in her tracks.

That's when we heard the plop.

'For the love of God!' Michael cried, cowpat dripping all over his designer shoes. 'I HATE this village!'

Everyone laughed as the policeman wrinkled his nose and bundled Michael in the car.

Tim hovered behind, unsure what to do with himself. I looked over and locked eyes with him. 'Better get used to this,' I called, and pointed to everyone on the green having fun. In amongst the crowd Owen and Izzy were throwing cakes in sheer and utter delight. ''Cos when I start your school in September . . .' I trailed off – there was no need to say anything else. I gave Tim a little wave and he went bright red.

The three council officials rushed to shake Mr Pringle-Bliss's hand as the police car drove away. 'You did it!' they all cried. One of them gestured to the hundreds and hundreds of villagers and tourists embroiled in the cake fight. '*This* is "significant historical value", right here.'

Jimmy and Martin ran up to me and we all high-fived. My face hurt from smiling so much. I couldn't remember when I'd ever been this happy.

Jimmy wiped cake off his glasses and cleared his throat. 'I'm – I'm sorry I didn't hang out with you as much,' he said to me. 'After your dad died.'

'Me too,' Martin said softly. I went quiet at that, and stared at the ground.

'I just didn't know what to say to you,' Jimmy said.

I shrugged. 'No one did.'

Jimmy and Martin looked sad, so I ignored the face pain and gave them a smile. We were friends now – that's all that mattered. All three of us ducked as cake flew through the air above us.

Mum hugged Grandad Barry in delight. 'Looks like Port Bren *is* going to be known for my God-awful cakes, after all,' she said.

Simon kissed Mum on the forehead and placed an arm round me.

Grandad Barry slapped him on the back. 'Not bad for a mainlander,' he smiled, and spat like he always did. But it wasn't in disgust this time. More like awe, actually.

Mr Pringle-Bliss smoothed down his blazer and walked over to the TV reporter. He whispered in his ear, and the reporter nodded and smiled. 'Six o'clock news, here I come,' he said to himself. He turned to the camera and flashed his best smile. 'Despite Port Bren's failure to officially break the world's tallest cake record,' the TV reporter said into the camera, 'it *can* still claim its fiftieth record in a week, and a place in history, as host to the world's biggest cake fight. It's like *La Tomatina*, but with baked goods.'

THWACK! He was caught in the crossfire and soon covered in cake. The newspaper reporter from *Jersey Journal* stood to the side, cake in his hands, clearly jealous of the TV reporter's scoop of the century.

The TV reporter wiped the goo from his face, ever the professional. 'One thing's for sure,' he continued as calmly as he could. 'They may have lost the battle, but they've won the war. They've saved their little village, and earned a little place in all our hearts in the process.' He looked lovingly at the villagers.

THWACK! He was hit in the face with a slab of cake.

More and more tourists flooded into the village bringing cake with them, desperate to join in the madness. The sky was full of flying flapjacks and coconut cake and apple crumble and chocolate gateau and ginger cake and lemon meringue and strawberry shortcake and blueberry pie and Yule log and upside-down cake, but nobody could tell if that was the right way up or not. It didn't seem as if it was ever going to stop. It. Was. Brilliant.

Six Months Later

Dad had always said that not everyone was a natural record breaker, and he was right – there's only ever been one Robert Wadlow. But *he* didn't really have to do anything, apart from being born tall.

Dad also said that not everyone had the courage, or the talent, or the sheer determination to do whatever it took to be the best. And there, he was absolutely one hundred per cent wrong.

When Simon first came to the village he said that people can break records for all sorts of things because half the time they don't realize how talented and unique and special they really are. I didn't believe him at first. But when I saw – when we absolutely *had* to be – just how determined and unique and special *we* were, I knew he was right. Port Bren might not have had the tallest, or the strongest, or the hungriest people – OK, apart from Trevor – but we did whatever we could to succeed. Nothing was going to stop us from trying to save our homes. And, thanks to the cake fight – *my* cake fight – everything had changed for the better.

Jimmy and Martin always come over to mine to play and at secondary school Jordan, Izzy, Owen and I are all friends. We hang round all the time, even though I'm still a year younger than them. I even help them with their maths homework sometimes.

Grandad Barry and Gwyn are now boyfriend and girl-friend. Gwyn hadn't told Grandad Barry yet, but she was hoping to propose to him on his next birthday. She didn't even care that Grandad Barry no longer wore a toupee, even for special occasions.

Frome Tourist still lodges with us, because he said that Port Bren was the nicest place he'd ever been on holiday. Port Bren is the *only* place he'd ever been on holi-day, but no one quibbled over that. He and Steve, the Olympic weightlifter from the Tower of Cake, are boyfriend and boyfriend now, but Mum said I wasn't to bang on about it.

Mum. Now, there's a story. After we'd saved Port Bren with all the cake and Grandad Barry's toupee and the odd Jersey Royal potato and packet of couscous being thrown, Simon asked Mum to marry him. And she said yes! And, honestly, it felt nice being a family again. I know that Simon will never replace Dad, but he's a good stepdad. I don't even care that I, Luke David, now have two first names. And having Sir Walter all the time is ace too. As an added bonus, Mr Pringle-Bliss named him as Port Bren's official mascot. Not quite Governor of Jersey, mind.

Because the cake fight had been so much fun we decided to make it an annual thing, just like *La Tomatina*. Mr Pringle-Bliss and the council had gone all out and ordered brand-new bunting for us, so when Port Bren's next Annual Cake Fight comes round we now no longer have to use the national-flag-of-Ghana banners, which is nice. And because we're famous now, we decided to twin our village with somewhere else in the world. After much debate – and Grandad Barry protesting that we'd be twinned with Wig Town in Scotland over his dead body – we settled on Bake in Cornwall, because that's what we did.

I personally wanted to twin with Pratt's Bottom in Kent, but Mum said that now he's left town for good, the village didn't need any more reminders of Michael, thank you very much.

Because he lives with us, Simon told me that we could talk about records anytime I wanted as Mum didn't mind now. Except I don't really want to any more. In fact, I've taken down all the posters from my bedroom wall, and I don't *have* to have any new record book that comes out. I just don't need to.

But what I did was this. My own personal record book

about how we saved Port Bren with cake and other household goods. Better than the *Port Bren Bible*, I think you'll agree. And who knows – maybe someday I'll even add glow-in-the-dark pictures to it.

PORT BREN'S 74 PROPOSED WORLD RECORD ATTEMPTS

1. Most doughnuts eaten in one minute – Trevor   Pass
2. Most chocolate bars eaten in one minute – Lydia   Fail
                (allergic to chocolate)
3. Most hula hoops hula-hooped in one minute – Gwyn   Pass
4. Loudest burp – Martin   Pass
5. Loudest scream – Gareth   Pass
                (unintentional)
6.   Oldest person – Absurdly Old Dave   Pass
7. Oldest person on Twitter – Absurdly Old Dave   Pass
8. Highest baton toss – Victoria   Pass
9. Longest time in office while dead – Basil Worsley   Pass
                (posthumous)
10. Largest volume of custard poured – Nikki Worsley   Pass
    down trousers   (bicycle-clipped to avoid spillage)
11. Most T-shirts worn – Jimmy   Pass
12. Most T-shirts worn by a cat – Mrs Jenkins' cat   Pass
13. Furthest distance in a canoe – Mr Wilson   Fail
                (he got lost)
14. Longest time to play dead – Seb   Fail
                (kept wandering off for food)
15. Longest continual chorus – Daffydd and the male choir   Pass
16. Most dogs washed in one hour – Port Bren Brownies   Fail
17. Highest dart score – Port Bren Darts Club   Fail
18. Fastest time to fry an egg on a unicycle – Port Bren   Fail
    Unicycle Club
19. Heaviest weight of paper shredded in one hour – Villagers   Pass

20. Fastest time to race down stairs on an – Anil   Fail
    inflatable dingy   (wasn't inflated)
21. Fastest time to put on a duvet – Mrs Renoir   Fail
22. Greasiest sausage – Pope Eggs Benedict Café   Pass
23. Longest dog – Gareth's Doberman   Pass
    (once the dog stayed still)
24. Most punches thrown in one minute – Grandad Barry   Fail
    (not as fit as he thought)
25. Furthest bounce on a space hopper – Sarah Fielding   Pass
26. Longest time spent in a bath of baked beans – Mrs Fielding   Pass
    (it runs in the family)
27. Fastest wheelbarrow race – Martin's brother   Pass
    (weak wrists don't run in the family)
28. Most marshmallows held in the mouth – Richard   Pass
    (thirty-two marshmallows)
29. Fewest marshmallows held in the mouth – Judy   Void
    (no marshmallows - not an actual record)
30. Fastest return of a homing pigeon – Frank   Fail
    (they didn't return. And they weren't pigeons)
31. Fastest time to mow the lawn – Col. Marsh   Pass
32. Oldest recipient of an ASBO – Col. Marsh   Pass
    (aged ninety-two. For mowing the lawn in the nude)
33. Recreating Pamplona's Running of the Bulls – Glyn   Void
    (not an actual record)
34. Fastest time to milk a cow – Adam Leroux   Pass
35. Fastest time to drink a pint of ale – Nigel   Pass
36. Fastest time to drink a pint of whiskey – Gordon   Pass
37. Fastest time to drink a pint of paint – Ken   Void
    (health and safety)
38. Fastest time to change a car tyre – Bill the mechanic   Pass
39. Fastest all-over spray tan – Very Orange Kat   Pass

40. Fastest all-over sunburn – Very Pale Pat .... Void
(health and safety)

41. Fastest time to serve fifty customers – Jane the cashier .... Pass

42. Tallest memorial statue – Port Bren High Street .... Pass

43. Fastest time to read 'War and Peace' – Barbara's Book Club .... Pass

44. Fastest time to travel 100m in a – Wheelie Good Darren .... Pass
wheelie bin

45. Smallest golf course – Douglas 'Tiger' Woods .... Pass
(no holes, three flags)

46. Longest time upright on a surf board – Andrew .... Pass

47. Fastest time to ice a cupcake – Josanne .... Pass

48. Fastest time to string up 100 yards of bunting – Mrs Wilson .... Pass

49. Fastest haircut – Wonky-eared Mo .... Pass

50. Fastest time to eat a pizza – Big-mouthed Bo .... Pass

51. Longest toenail clippings – Giant-toed Flo .... Pass

52. Longest bike jump – Owen .... Pass

53. Fastest time to drink a – The Other Barry .... Not Attempted
bottle of ketchup

54. Fastest time to drive 1000m – Lindsey D. .... Fail
(Port Bren has clear rules. Nothing above 10mph)

55. Longest continual game of – Port Bren Lawn Bowls Club .... Pass
lawn bowls (four days)

56. Fastest time to sing Jersey – Kathy Marphatt .... Pass
national anthem

57. Most toads licked in one hour – John Adams .... Fail
(hospitalised due to one toad being poisonous)

58. Fastest time to superglue hand to head – Ben .... Void
(health and safety)

59. Fastest time to carve a turkey – Roy Fort the butcher .... Pass

60. Loudest note on a party blower – the butcher's son .... Pass

61. Most buses caught in one day – Amy Willis .... Fail
(Port Bren bus only comes once a week)

62. Longest distance to pull a bus by your ear – Mitch   Pass
(only just. Port Bren bus only comes once a week, and he nearly missed it)

63. Fastest time around the village in a barrel – T. Bayley   Fail
(couldn't fit in barrel)

64. Most freckles on face – Jersey Journal Reporter   Pass
(unintentional)

65. Longest stand-up comedy – Mike 'the Comic' Comertron   Fail
routine   (seventy-two hours, but jokes could
not be classified as 'comedy')

66. Most dominoes toppled in a chain reaction – Megan   Fail
(one million dominoes attempted; could not find enough dominoes)

67. Most body parts pierced in one hour – Biker Phil   Fail
(fainted after first piercing)

68. Highest number of bees worn in a beard of bees – Sophie   Pass

69. Longest time to hold on – Miles 'Mutton Buster' Leroux   Pass
to a galloping sheep

70. Most scones eaten in one hour – Molly   Pass
(eighty-seven scones)

71. Most peas stabbed on a fork – Michela   Pass

72. Most snails worn on face – Jodie   Fail
(doesn't like snails)

73. World's oldest pot of jam (unopened) – Pam   Pass

74. Most wine glasses smashed during an opera song – Jill   Incomplete

Also noted:

Longest ear hair – Lloyd Blenkinsop   Void

Did not count towards Port Bren target (record set in 1981)

Acknowledgements

My heartfelt thanks to everyone at Random House Children's Books for publishing the book and supporting it, and me, with such enthusiasm. What marvellous people you all are. Particular thanks to Annie Eaton, Natalie Doherty, and to Becky Stradwick for her invaluable notes ('Ramp up the crazy!') and hilariously encouraging emails.

To my agent and fellow SHSG alumnus, Jodie Marsh at United Agents, for her patience, skill and support – and for believing in me in the first place.

Thanks to Michael Whitty and everyone at the Guinness World Records London headquarters for their help and insight.

To the London College of Communication's MA Screenwriting Class of 2008. Where would I be without all your workshop advice and feedback? Hollywood, probably.

To my wonderful friends, who have always supported me through thick and thin. Except those who haven't. Particular mention to Nicola, Amy and Katie for their completely uninspiring pep talks.

And finally, thanks to my family, especially my mum, dad and brother, who have shaped me into the person and writer I am today. Nice to have someone to blame for all my shortcomings.